Boston Christmas Miracles

*Rediscovering the magic of Christmas…
and finding love!*

It's Christmas on the Boston Beacon Hospital
children's ward, and these pediatric doctors and
nurses are doing their very best to bring hope to
so many families…but will their own wishes be
coming true? Whether it's a warmhearted nurse
melting the icy reserves of a sexy single dad, a jilted
canine-therapy nurse wondering if Santa can deliver
miracles, a trainee doc who's home all alone until
an old flame comes knocking, or a night of passion
with unexpected consequences for the grumpiest
surgeon, will working together to help the small
patients on Ward 34 make its staff realize this really
is the most wonderful time of the year…for love?

Grab a hot chocolate and join us for…

The Nurse's Holiday Swap by Ann McIntosh
A Puppy on the 34th Ward by Juliette Hyland

Available now!

And look out for…

Home Alone with the Children's Doctor
by Traci Douglass
A Surgeon's Christmas Baby
by Deanne Anders

Coming soon!

Dear Reader,

Writing a holiday story for Harlequin has been a dream of mine for as long as I can remember. I used to sneak these books off my mother's shelf. My sister and I discussed our favorite holiday continuities, and calling to tell her that it was happening is a core memory!

Dr. Nick Walker is a motivated, kind and caring overachiever whose successes aren't enough for his wildly successful family. He is a hero truly worthy of the title who can't see the real man in the mirror. Through Bryn's love he finally recognizes that his achievements are amazing in their own right.

Bryn Bedford has spent her life pleasing everyone and has almost nothing to show for it. This holiday season, she's determined to ignore the holiday she used to love and just get by with her cute therapy dog, Honey. Enter Nick Walker to upend all her plans. Can he help her find the holiday spirit she's lost…and the love she craves?

Juliette Hyland

A PUPPY ON THE 34ᵀᴴ WARD

JULIETTE HYLAND

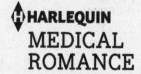

HARLEQUIN
MEDICAL
ROMANCE

Special thanks and acknowledgment are given to Juliette Hyland for her contribution to the Boston Christmas Miracles miniseries.

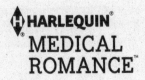

Recycling programs
for this product may
not exist in your area.

ISBN-13: 978-1-335-59505-8

A Puppy on the 34th Ward

Copyright © 2023 by Harlequin Enterprises ULC

For questions and comments about the quality of this book, please contact us at CustomerService@Harlequin.com.

Harlequin Enterprises ULC
22 Adelaide St. West, 41st Floor
Toronto, Ontario M5H 4E3, Canada
www.Harlequin.com

Printed in U.S.A.

Juliette Hyland began crafting heroes and heroines in high school. She lives in Ohio with her Prince Charming, who has patiently listened to many rants regarding characters failing to follow the outline. When not working on fun and flirty happily-ever-afters, Juliette can be found spending time with her beautiful daughters, giant dogs or sewing uneven stitches with her sewing machine.

Books by Juliette Hyland

Harlequin Medical Romance
Neonatal Nurses
A Nurse to Claim His Heart

The Pediatrician's Twin Bombshell
Reawakened at the South Pole
The Vet's Unexpected Houseguest
The Prince's One-Night Baby
Rules of Their Fake Florida Fling
Redeeming Her Hot-Shot Vet
Tempted by Her Royal Best Friend

Visit the Author Profile page at Harlequin.com.

For my team—you guys know the reasons!

**Praise for
Juliette Hyland**

"A delightful second chance on love with intriguing characters, powerful back stories and tantalizing chemistry! Juliette Hyland quickly catches her reader's attention…. I really enjoyed their story! I highly recommend this book…. The story line has a medical setting with a whole lot of feels in the mix!"

—*Goodreads* on *Falling Again for the Single Dad*

CHAPTER ONE

"LIKE THE DECORATIONS?"

A staffer Dr. Nick Walker didn't know smiled brightly as they hung another pretend candy along the corridor of Ward 34.

He nodded, though the truth was that he didn't really care for holiday decor. "Quite festive."

"We're adding a few new things this year."

"I'm sure it will look great." The kids who had to visit the pediatric wing during Christmastime would love it. Anything to make little ones and their parents, who'd rather be anywhere else, happy was good with Nick.

However, he had no way of determining if this year was grander than the last. Since completing his residency, he'd spent no more than two years in any one place.

And today was his first full day at Boston Beacon Hospital. So the clock was already ticking. He might see Ward 34's decor next year, but after that...

His chest tightened at the thought of moving,

even if it was his choice now. As a military kid, he'd moved almost every two years as his father had chased bigger and bigger assignments. Nick had lived in four countries and eight states at thirty-six.

Part of him always wondered if this was the last place.

Boston was nice. But so were most cities. That was one lesson he'd learned moving his things from one part of the world to another: Find out what made each place tick. Locate the best pizza joint, the ideal coffee hub and at least one fun hole-in-the-wall only the locals knew about, and anywhere could feel like home.

For a while at least.

"Dr. Walker." Dr. Javi Pascal raised his hand as he walked over with a young woman. A new hire… Nick knew the routine. He'd been introduced after his orientation last week.

"Dr. Nick Walker, this is Nurse Ailani Kekoa."

"Nice to meet you." Nick offered his hand. He'd been the new person in so many places— he understood the nerves. Not that the nurse with the bright smile looked nervous.

"Nick is our newest pediatrician," Javi continued. "Today is his first day on the floor, in fact."

"I guess that means you can't recommend any good restaurants or coffee shops?" Ailani gestured out the window to the Boston skyline.

"Fraid not," he offered without following her

gaze. The Boston skyline was beautiful, but it was just another city, another layover point in life. "But if you hear of any, let me know."

"I'm sure my roommate will tire of me peppering her with questions, but if I find any, I'll pass them along. Newbies help each other out, right?"

"Right."

"Oh, I see another doctor..."

"That's my cue." Ailani waved goodbye as she followed Javi down the hallway.

Nick turned his attention back to the tablet chart. He had four patients he needed to see before lunch, and one was being discharged. Always a good day.

He clicked two more buttons, then felt pressure against his legs. Looking down, Nick blinked twice as the golden retriever wagged its tail. As a pediatrician, he was used to little ones grabbing his leg.

The occasional sibling getting loose from their understandably exhausted parents.

A dog, dressed as a Christmas tree and wearing a star headband, rubbed its nose against his leg again. This was a first.

"Honey!" The thick Boston accent was attached to one of the most beautiful women he'd ever seen.

"Sorry—Honey doesn't normally wander." The white woman made several hand gestures, and the dog sat, then lay at her feet.

Her green eyes met his, and Nick found himself at a loss for words. He'd connected with a few people in his nomadic life, but he'd never met someone and felt this gut punch.

The woman cleared her throat, and Nick shook his head. "Sorry—it's my first day on the floor."

"Bryn Bedford." She held out her hand, and Nick clasped it. The connection was brief but somehow intense.

Not that that made any sense.

"Nick Walker."

"Nice to meet you, Nick. This naughty one is Honey."

He pursed his lips as he looked at the dog. He hated being the bearer of bad news, but dogs—even ones dressed in such cute regalia—weren't technically allowed.

"It's nice to meet Honey, and she is adorable, particularly in her tree outfit." He cleared his throat. "But this is a hospital."

"Really?" Bryn's green eyes sparkled as he stated the obvious. Then she bent and lifted the tree, showing off the patch on the back that said Therapy Dog.

"Honey is one of the Paws for Hope therapy dogs."

"And dressed as a Christmas tree?"

Bryn laughed, a sound that seemed to go straight to his soul. "I'm afraid that's my fault. She loves dressing up, and I lose all willpower when I see a cute dog outfit. I think she has more outfits than I do. In fact, I know that's true as my closet is more than half hers, and I'm the one that buys the outfits.

"My…" She paused and looked at Honey. When she looked back at Nick, a bit of the sparkle had left her eyes. "Someone once told me I treat her as a dress-up doll."

She spoke to Honey, "But it's just because you are so cute."

The dog was adorable… Bryn even more so. "I've not had much interaction with therapy animals."

"Do you have a few minutes? I can show you what Honey can do. I'm scheduled to see Lucas before he's discharged."

"Lucas is on my rounds list, so why don't we go together?"

"Great." Bryn and Honey walked beside him.

"What support is Honey offering Lucas? I thought therapy dogs were usually here to see patients that were stuck here for a while. Discharge day is usually one of the best days."

"Usually." Bryn sighed as she rubbed a hand over Honey's head. "But one of Lucas's moms is in the army. They were being PC—something, it means *moved…*"

"PCS'd. Permanent Change of Station." It was a phrase Nick had heard so often around the dinner table. His father's life had revolved around receiving PCS orders. Once his siblings had gone into the military, they'd sent notes to the family group chat every time a new location had come in.

A group chat they'd kicked him out of when he'd left West Point Military Academy before his second year to pursue his own dreams.

Or quit…according to his father.

His life was the only one not controlled by orders. And yet he hadn't put down permanent roots.

"That's it! PCS'd. They were moving cross country when the appendicitis struck. It's why he's here and not at a base hospital somewhere. And his mom had to head onto her… I want to say office. That's not right, though. Starts with a *D*." Bryn tapped on her forehead, like she was trying to pull the phrase from her brain.

This was another phrase Nick could provide. "Duty station."

"You know all the lingo. That will help."

Bryn's words were bright, but Nick wasn't sure. Sure, he knew military lingo, but helping a kid sad about moving…there were no quick fixes for that.

"So Honey is along to cheer him up."

Bryn shook her head. "I prefer to think of it as Honey is here to offer what Lucas needs. She can give cuddles, pets, a soft place to cry. Or cheer, if that's what the patient needs."

Nick looked at the happy golden, its tail wagging as the star bounced on her headband. She looked cheerful, but he knew that not every patient was ready for cheer. Even one getting ready for discharge. "That is a nice thought."

"Honey has been a therapy dog for two years. She's quite skilled at recognizing what patients need."

"And how long have you been a therapy-dog handler?" The door to Lucas's room came into view. Nick had moments left with Bryn Bedford—and he wanted to savor all of them.

"Honey is my first therapy dog."

"What did you do beforehand?"

An emotion passed over Bryn's eyes that sent a knife to his heart.

How often had someone asked him something personal and he panicked? He was the black sheep of his family, the one who'd "refused" to serve his country, at least according to his father. The general had never seen a life outside of uniform as serving, never seen his children as more than an extension of his success.

All of that added up to a ton of questions Nick never answered. If one got trophies for creative ways to change topics, he'd have a wall full of gold.

"We've arrived." He made too big of a gesture as they got to Lucas's door. But he wanted her to feel comfortable, get them back on the easy footing they'd had before he'd dug too deep.

"So we have." Bryn's green eyes met his before she looked at Honey. "Shall we let this girl go first?"

"Sure." Nick was curious to see the dog in action. Most of his interactions with dogs were as service animals. Working dogs.

Honey was a working dog, but it was different. Her role was comfort.

"Hi, Lucas. Can Honey come in?"

Giving a choice. Nick smiled. That was something so many adults forgot to offer children.

"Yes!" The little boy's voice was bright as he patted the bed.

Honey looked at Bryn, who motioned with her hand, then jumped up and put two paws on the bed.

Lucas leaned over and kissed the top of Honey's head. "I'm leaving today. So I won't see you again." He said the words, then sucked back a sob.

How many times had Nick done that as a child? *Be strong, never quit* was the family motto.

"I don't see a lot of people again." Lucas's words were whispered, but his mother heard them.

Bryn stepped to his mother's side and offered her a hand. The woman squeezed it as she stood a little taller.

"I know it's rough, Lucas, but Fort Drum will be fun. It gets lots of snow." His mother's bright smile didn't quite reach her eyes, but it was clear she was trying to do her best.

The boy said nothing as he leaned his head against Honey's.

"I'm Dr. Walker."

"You're here so I can go to Fort Drum?"

"Yes." Nick stepped close and got down, so his face was eye level with Lucas. "My dad was in the army."

Lucas's head popped up. "You moved a lot?"

"Every two years." Nick hit the watch on his hand. "Like clockwork. I've lived all over the world."

"My mom has only been stateside, never OCO-NUS."

OCONUS—outside the Continental United States. A phrase only a military kid understood.

"My dad was everywhere."

But never at home.

Those were words that did not need to be spoken.

His father had focused on his career. And only his career. And his mother, a career diplomat, had been gone nearly as much. The fact that they'd had four children when they'd spent years separated by continents was a miracle.

Besides, Nick's experience was not the path that most members of the armed forces chose.

He'd watched many fathers and mothers in uniform pick up their kids from school. Attend school plays, do all the things civilian parents did.

"It's not fun to move, is it?"

"No." Lucas's lip trembled as his hand stroked Honey's soft coat.

The dog shifted a paw and looked at him. Nick could swear she understood all the words, though rationally he knew Honey was likely just responding to the tension in the young one.

"But this is the last one." Lucas looked to his mother, who nodded.

"The last one?"

"Mom is retiring after this station. She says we're staying in Watertown. That's next to Fort Drum. She grew up there." He sighed as he bopped Honey's nose.

"That's great. So one more new place, one more new school." Nick grinned. The last location was the best news a family constantly on military orders could get.

He'd met a few kids whose parents followed Lucas's mom's path—did their best to land their last duty location as close to home as possible.

"Where was the last place for you?"

There wasn't one. Not really. Though Nick knew what Lucas was asking.

"DC." The District of Columbia. His father had stationed at the Pentagon as the chairman of the joint chiefs of staff, literally incapable of achieving more in his career. His mother, not to be outdone, had spent the final years of her life rising in the ranks of the State Department, both more comfortable in White House briefings than their living room.

"Shall we look at your incision now?"

"Can Honey stay?"

Nick looked to Bryn, her smile eating away at the homesickness the conversation with Lucas had unintentionally brought on. "Can she?"

"Of course." Bryn stepped toward the bed. "But she needs to be at your feet while Dr. Walker looks at your belly."

Bryn snapped out a quick rhythm, and Honey pulled her paws off the bed, then jumped up and curled at Lucas's feet. A golden blanket over his legs.

Lifting his shirt, Lucas pointed to the three holes in his lower abdomen. "I've seen so many doctors. Even one I wasn't supposed to!"

Nick looked at Lucas's mother with a raised brow.

"A Dr. Murphy stopped in this morning. I think he meant to be in a different room. He was a tad flustered."

"Dr. Murphy is one of our surgeons. Always busy."

Bryn's voice was light, but Nick heard the unstated: *Great with kids, but a little gruff if you aren't his patient.*

"Why do so many doctors have to look at me?"

Nick let out a chuckle and motioned for Lucas to lower his shirt. "Well, your surgeon checks you out because he yanked out that yucky appendix using a special technique called laparoscopic surgery. I'm a pediatrician. That means I specialize in children's medicine. The hospital just wants to make sure you get to see everyone."

"So you don't get sued."

"Lucas!" His mother crossed her arms.

The little one hung his head, and Honey sat up so he could rub between her ears. "Sorry."

The mumbled word wasn't heartfelt, but Nick didn't mind.

"You're going to be sore for another week or so. If you notice anything coming out of the holes, if they itch or hurt really bad, you need to tell one of your moms, all right?"

Lucas nodded, not looking away from the therapy dog.

"The wounds are already scabbing on the edges. That's a wonderful sign. Infection is rare, but if he spikes a fever over a hundred and one, take him to the ER. Otherwise, a nurse will be in shortly with discharge papers, and you'll be on your way."

His mom nodded and moved to Lucas's side. "Time to say goodbye to Honey now."

He leaned over the bed, gripped the dog's neck

and let out a soft cry. "Bye, Honey. I'll try to remember you."

The phrase tore through Nick. He'd said exactly those words or heard them whispered through tears as a friend whose name and a face were gone from his memory had hugged him.

The life of a kid on the move.

"But this is the last stop." Nick offered the boy a smile but knew it didn't heal the hurt he felt right now.

Nick looked at Lucas's mom. "Good luck. I hope you enjoy the snow."

"We do." She ran her hand through Lucas's hair. "All right, sweetheart, you need to let Honey do her job and go see others."

Lucas squeezed her one more time, then pulled back. "Bye, Honey."

"It was nice to meet you." Bryn snapped her fingers again, and Honey padded to her side. Bryn picked up her leash, straightened Honey's star headband and headed for the door.

Nick followed. "Honey was great in there."

"She usually is." Bryn ran her hand along the dog's head. "However, you were the actual star. If her headband wasn't covered in dog fur, I'd offer it to you. You've really lived all over?"

"Four countries and eight states."

"Wow." She shook her head. "I've been in Boston my whole life."

"The accent kind of gives that away." Nick

grinned, enjoying the tilt of her head and the fiery expression crossing her green eyes a little too much.

"*I* don't have an accent. You do."

"Of course." He laughed, enjoying the interaction. Bryn was gorgeous in her bright holiday sweater, with a sweet golden retriever at her heels. Picture perfect...and Nick was the furthest thing from it.

"I'm off to see Susie Cole. They admitted her last night. Do you want to see if she likes dogs, too?" The question was out before he thought it through. He was working. It was his first day, but he was hoping Bryn and Honey would tag along.

She looked at her phone, pulling up the note tracker. "Susie is on my list."

"List?"

"Yes. Honey is the goodest girl." Her tone shifted up, and Honey's ears tipped up, too.

Nick wasn't even sure Bryn was aware of the tonal shift.

She looked at him, and the hit of recognition rocked through him again. There was something about this woman that called to him.

Maybe he was just lonelier than he wanted to admit. He'd stayed in Phoenix for almost eighteen months. Gotten close to his colleagues, even briefly considered staying. But his mind refused to settle, so he'd set off again.

The military kid unable to stay still, even though he'd refused to wear the uniform.

That must've been it. The reason his mind was reaching for connection.

"Intake makes sure the patients and their grown-ups are comfortable with therapy-dog visits. You don't know about allergies or what home life is like. If a child fears dogs, it doesn't matter how sweet Honey is, that will just upset them." Bryn shrugged. "And if their grown-ups don't want them around dogs for whatever reason, you want to honor that."

"Their grown-ups?" She'd said that twice.

"Not everyone has parents." Lines pulled at the corners of her eyes, and her smile faltered a little.

Families came in all shapes and sizes. His family was technically what most people thought of. A mom and dad, with quite a few siblings, but it was far from picture perfect. "I always use the term *guardians*."

"That's good. But if a sister or brother raises you, or an aunt or grandparent... I don't know, a teacher friend of mine uses it in her classes, and I stole it."

They'd arrived at Susie's room. That wasn't a surprise. The pediatric wing took up the entire second floor, but it didn't take long to walk between areas. Still, he craved more time with the woman beside him.

Yep, loneliness was setting in. Luckily, Nick

had a lifetime of learning how to deal with that. When he got home, he'd pop in one of his favorite movies, grab some popcorn and a soda, and chill.

"Ready?" Bryn's smile was perfection, and he had to take a deep breath.

Focus.

"Of course."

Bryn cut her eyes to Nick as they walked through Susie's door. The new doctor was the most attractive man she'd ever seen. His deep brown eyes seemed to peer right through her.

He looked like he belonged on the set of television drama. The kind where every doctor was hot as hell and the entire floor was dating each other. Drama and lifesaving antics happening constantly and all wrapped up nicely in an hour.

Or at least by the end of the two-part special.

Life wasn't that way. There was a reason so many books, blogs and Human Resources pamphlets recommended not dating in the workplace.

Not that Bryn needed reminding. One doctor ex-husband was more than enough.

Her thumb slipped to her empty ring finger. Almost a year since her marriage had ended. Two days into her honeymoon.

For reasons Ethan had never fully explained but that had basically boiled down to her not being "the right fit." A harsh statement considering how much of herself she'd seemed to bottle up during their relationship.

"Puppy!" Susie's bright call broke through the unhappy memories.

The little one looked tired but not nearly as sick as her intake form indicated. Bryn didn't get many details, but as Ward 34's part-time therapy-dog handler, she had the basics.

And since she was a registered nurse, she could read between the lines better than most. She'd loved nursing. Another thing the implosion of her marriage had stolen.

Susie's blond curls were a mess, but her eyes were bright. No hint of the fainting that had brought her in.

"You look like you're feeling better this morning." Nick stepped next to Susie's bed.

"I want to go home." She stuck her bottom lip out and crossed her arms.

Her mother yawned, then frowned. "I know, Susie, but we have to find out why you fainted yesterday." The woman rubbed her hands together as she looked at Nick. "I'm Ellen. Susie's mom. I'm almost thinking I overreacted. It's been…been a year."

Honey nudged Bryn's leg, but she didn't release her. Dogs picked up on emotions, and it was clear that Ellen was deep in her feels. She had a daughter in the hospital, but that didn't explain the year comment.

If Ellen wanted to pet Honey, then she was more than welcome to, but Honey had to wait.

"Tell me a bit about what happened." Nick leaned against the wall, crossing his arms, his eyes fully directed at Ellen. Ready to take in the information.

Seriously, in blue scrubs with his stethoscope hanging from his pocket, the man was gorgeous.

"Mommy!" Susie looked over at Honey.

Nick looked at Bryn. "Can Honey sit with Susie while I talk to her mom?"

"Of course." Bryn dropped Honey's leash, then snapped out the release code she'd trained Honey with.

The golden wandered over to the bed, her tail wagging as she waited for Bryn to snap again, telling her it was okay to put two paws on the bed.

"My husband..." Ellen closed her eyes, taking a deep breath. "He's been gone."

"And he can't video chat," Susie interjected.

Ellen pursed her lips, then smiled at her daughter. "He's going to be so surprised at how much you've grown."

Her stance sent alarm bells through Bryn. How many times had her mother said something like that? *Daddy will be so surprised at how big you are. It's okay—his trip just took too long. He'll pick you up next weekend.*

It wasn't until she'd been almost a teen that she'd pushed back and called her father what he was. A deadbeat dad. A man who blew into her and her mother's life when he felt like it. And disappeared again when life got too hard or he met someone else who caught his fancy. Or when the system caught up with him for unpaid child support for her or the four half siblings she knew about.

"Anyway." Ellen looked at her daughter, then at Nick. "She was tired, but she's five. And while she doesn't nap anymore, sometimes…" She shrugged.

"Sometimes she needs one." Nick looked at Susie, making a silly face to head off the frustration Bryn could see in the girl's face. "I need one sometimes, too."

Susie's eyes narrowed, but then she refocused on Honey.

And this was why therapy animals were such a blessing. Calming influences that made life easier in one of the most difficult places in the world.

"I'm really starting to think I overreacted. That maybe she didn't faint…but I know she did. She was standing in the kitchen arguing over a snack."

"I wanted raisins."

"I like raisins." Nick laughed. "Especially the yogurt ones."

"I've never had those—Mommy!"

"We'll see."

"That means no," Susie whispered to Honey.

Nick's eyes found Bryn's as she covered her mouth to hide the smile.

"I'm going to check you out, Susie." He pulled the stethoscope from his pocket and showed it to her. "Do you know what this is?"

"It listens to my heart."

"It does." Nick nodded, his focus on the child. "Your lungs, too. I can even use it to listen to your stomach growl. Want to see?"

Bryn's heart melted as she watched him put the earpieces in Susie's ears, then drop the diaphragm to her belly.

"Wow."

As a nurse, she'd worked with so many specialties. There were dedicated professionals in all of them, but pediatricians had some of the best bedside manner she'd ever witnessed. It was outside the hospital, though, that you needed to focus on. Her ex-husband could put on a good show when he wanted to, too.

Nick took over and started checking Susie, explaining what he was doing to both the child and her mother. Answering questions without getting upset or frustrated.

A perfect bedside manner.

Which was why Ethan dismissing his tiny patients should have been one of so many red flags. But she'd wanted to believe it had been just because he'd been focused on his career, on climbing the ranks so he could make changes to benefit all patients.

A catchphrase he used to make himself look better. Though now she believed what he wanted was prestige. Not that it mattered. She wasn't his wife.

Not anymore.

"All right." Nick put his stethoscope back into his pocket and looked at Ellen. "The good news is she seems healthy. And the monitors last night caught nothing. Our night staff nurses said she did well."

"And the bad news?" Ellen's foot started tapping.

This was a woman well-versed in bad news. Her foot was tapping, but her shoulders were straight. Her face carefully devoid of expression.

"I don't know why she fainted. Sometimes episodes happen and we can't determine a reason. It never happens again, and it's a story that you tell her when she's a teen driving you up the wall."

"Other times?"

Nick looked at Susie, whose attention was focused on Honey. "Other times it takes another episode, or many episodes, for us to determine what's going on. I recommend following up with her pediatrician. If she faints again, has shortness of breath, chest pain, a fever over a hundred and one, bring her back." Nick shook his head, his shoulders dipping just a hair. "I'm sorry. I don't have a better answer. It could be stress. Children experience that just like adults."

"Yeah, well, there's enough of that to go around." Ellen caught a sob and shook her head. "Sorry."

"No need to apologize."

Bryn's eyes were getting misty as Nick comforted Ellen. She wasn't his patient, but the care in his voice, the extra time spent with her daughter, the acknowledgment that sometimes there wasn't an answer...

It was more than many doctors were willing to do.

The definition of a perfect doctor.

Bryn wanted to shake that thought from her mind. Nick was a good doctor...to the two patients she'd seen. That meant nothing. It was his first day on the floor of Ward 34.

She knew that stress, hard cases, rough days—those were when you really saw someone's character.

"If you have questions, let the discharge nurse know, and I'll come back. It was very nice to meet you, Susie."

"I love Honey."

"Me, too." Bryn smiled and nodded to Nick as he walked out the door. "Does your mom want to pet her before I go?"

Ellen let out a laugh that sounded a little too close to a sob as she sat beside Susie on the bed.

She ran her hands over Honey's head. Her shoulders relaxed, and the lines around her eyes disappeared as Honey worked her magic. "Thank you."

"This is Honey's dream job." The dog wagged her tail and dutifully stood as Bryn snapped three times and picked up her leash. Honey loved this, and Bryn loved helping people. Maybe she wasn't in nurse's scrubs now, but the thrill she got seeing Honey work made up for it.

Almost.

CHAPTER TWO

PULLING OFF HER COAT, Bryn tried to ignore the happy couples at each table as she slid to the bar seat. Myers + Chang was her favorite restaurant—it was also the perfect date night location. She came here by herself often. After years of almost never coming or having takeout, she refused to abandon her favorite place because she wasn't part of a couple.

She'd asked Ethan to come here with her so many times. Always getting her hopes up and then settling when he'd automatically refused. Three years and the man hadn't made such a simple thing a priority.

Never mind that she'd been willing to go where he'd wanted. Even for her birthday, he'd pouted, saying there was nothing he liked, and she'd canceled the reservations here and gone to the chain seafood place he preferred. Why was it, a year after they'd broken up, so easy to see what a terrible partner he'd been?

Because I wanted to believe that I'd found someone to stand by me.

After spending her teen years telling her mother she was better off alone than standing by her serial-cheater, disappearing husband, Bryn had believed she'd found happily ever after. A man with a stable job who wouldn't disappear on her. An illusion she'd clung to.

If her mother were alive, she'd apologize. It was easier to stay with less than you deserved than one realized.

Though Bryn had no intention of making the same mistake again.

Now she could eat here every night—though her pocketbook would balk at the idea.

Her phone buzzed, and she knew it was Indigo, a nursing friend from Brigham and Women's Hospital. The woman's annual holiday party was in a week. She and her husband threw a huge event. Decorations galore, people, spiked punch and a white-elephant gift exchange. Two years ago, they'd made the white-elephant exchange Bryn's bridal shower. And last year, everyone had been busy talking about the next steps for her and Ethan.

A year later, she was sitting alone at a bar. Divorced, living with a roommate, doing her best to avoid reminders that instead of celebrating her one-year anniversary, she was alone.

Still can't make it. Sorry.

She sent the text and set her phone down.

Ethan was Indigo's husband's best friend. Ethan would attend, despite hating parties, if for no other reason than to prove that the divorce didn't bother him…which it probably didn't. If she was honest, it wasn't dropping the two hundred pounds of dead weight that was her ex that bothered Bryn. It was everyone's questions. The not-so-quiet whispers, the pitying looks hidden not quick enough. It was just too much. So she was skipping Christmas this year.

The parties, the gifts, the gatherings…all of it. Maybe next year she'd pick back up the holiday traditions she'd enjoyed, but this year…nope.

"This is a busy place."

The words were smooth. Bryn couldn't stop the smile as she turned to find Nick.

"Nick. Or Dr. Walker."

"Nick, please." He grinned and shook a bit of rain from his hair. "I thought Boston got snow."

"We do." Bryn shrugged as she looked at the front doors. The rain wasn't hard, more of a mist than anything. "But most of it comes in January and February."

"So no white Christmas." Nick stepped closer as a couple moved behind him.

Her heart rate picked up, and her body coated with heat. He was fine. His full lips, dark skin, with just a hint of stubble on his chin. If she rubbed his jaw…

Bryn cut that thought off.

Nick was also a colleague. Which meant he was off-limits. *Fool me once, shame on you, fool me twice…*

Bryn had no intention of falling into the patterns that had burned her so badly.

"I can't tell you no white Christmas. It happens. But an icy Christmas or a cold, dry Christmas happen more often."

"Man, I thought I'd see my first white Christmas in years." Nick waved as the bartender stepped up.

"You getting a drink or eating at the bar?"

Nick's eyes slid to hers. "Do you mind if I join you?"

Yes. But only because he was so attractive. And she was already fantasizing about how he kissed. How his fingers might feel on her cheek.

Her skin prickled, but she could hardly tell him no because her body was awakening from the slumber she'd put it in after her divorce.

"Please." She gestured to the seat next to her. With any luck, he'd say or do something that pushed the sensitive, hot doc from her mind and let her focus on an undesirable trait.

Bryn wanted to slap the horrid thought from her mind. Nick had been perfectly nice. Her issues were not his.

"So, what's good here?"

Nick picked up the menu, and she tried not to focus on how close he was. That if she shifted just right, her knee would brush his.

Seriously, maybe it was time to break out the dating apps. Though the very idea made her insides twist.

"Why did you choose this place?" Bryn looked at the menu in his hand. It was all good. The owners even had their own cookbooks. She'd tried a few of the recipes at home. They were good, but it wasn't the same.

"It's busy."

"'It's busy.' Nick. You walked in here because it was busy?" She laughed and leaned toward him before pulling herself back. "That's the whole reason? Do you like dim sum? Or fried rice, or ramen?" Myers + Chang was delicious, but if those weren't things his palate enjoyed…

"I'm not a picky eater. And yes, I chose it because it was busy. First rule of AreaFam—pay attention to what the locals like."

"AreaFam?"

"Area familiarization. It's a term my father used when we got to new places." A look passed over his eyes before Nick smiled at her. "If you move every few years, you figure out how to fit in. At least as much as possible."

"Makes sense. The nasi goreng is my favorite

dish. It's a Southeast Asian fried rice and wicked good."

"Wicked." Nick tried to place the right inflection on the word, but it sounded off.

"Almost."

"That's a lie." Nick's smile lit up their little area of the bar, and Bryn giggled.

"It is. That was terrible." The term was one most Bostonians learned before they were two. It was also a word many associated with the city and tried to replicate. Usually without success.

"Give it time." Bryn winked, but the atmosphere around Nick shifted. Like time wasn't in his favor. The feeling made little sense—she was reading into things. Something she did far too often.

"Ready, Bryn?" The bartender, Bill, smiled as he stood in front of them.

A way to shift the topic—perfect. She pushed the menu that she hadn't needed to look at across the bar. "I'll have nasi goreng and a sangria, please."

"And you?" Bill looked at Nick, who peeked at the menu before handing it back to him.

"Nasi goreng for me too, and the pineapple-ginger soda with tequila please."

"So you enjoy moving?" Bryn loved the idea of travel, but she'd never ventured very far. She'd grown up in Boston, gotten her registered nursing degree at Boston College, then started working at Brigham and Women's Hospital. Her entire life had revolved around the city.

It was a good life. This was home. Even when the world collapsed on itself.

"Not really."

She must have made a face because Nick shrugged and leaned back, his features closing off a little.

"I just feel like I have to." He nodded to Bill as he dropped the drinks off.

"Have to?" There was a tone in his voice, an ache that pierced through the hum of the restaurant. She laid her hand on his, squeezing it, then pulling back. "What does that mean?"

His eyes shifted, looking at the minimal space between their hands. Was his hand burning like hers? Did he want to reach over and hold her, like she yearned to do with him?

"I don't know." Nick picked up his drink, took a sip, then shifted so his hand was on the back of his seat.

So she couldn't reach for him again?

"I just… I don't know what home feels like. Never found a place that fit."

"No family home?" Even with a family on the move, there had to be somewhere they all congregated. Except there didn't. So many families never met up.

She and her mother had had dinner every Sunday before she'd passed, more out of obligation than love. And her father… Bryn wasn't even sure what state he was in. Hell, the man could've left the mortal plane and she wouldn't know.

"Nope. My father retired from the service but leads a big military consulting firm in DC. He technically has a condo in downtown DC, but in reality, he lives at the office."

"Wow." Bryn loved nursing. Being a therapy-dog handler was nice, too. Though it didn't quite fill the hole the same. But she wouldn't live at the hospital. Balance was too important.

"Yeah. The man is a certified workaholic. He got worse when Mom passed a few years ago." Nick reached for his drink, took a bigger sip, then set it aside. "And my siblings take after dad. All of them."

"All of them?" She'd begged her mother for a sibling when she'd been younger, not realizing that her father would need to be home…or her mother would need to choose another love to make that happen. Still, she'd always wanted a big family.

"Youngest of four!" Nick laughed as he pointed to himself. "And they live all over. My oldest brother is stationed at PACOM in Hawaii. My other brother is Special Forces, and who knows where he's at right now. And my sister was a fighter pilot, but she wants to keep climbing the ranks, so she's not in the cockpit anymore. She's at Wright-Patterson in Ohio, doing something she can't talk about. So family gatherings and home aren't really what the Walkers aim for.

"But you." Nick leaned over, but his hand didn't come closer to hers. "You're a homegrown Bostonian."

"Never left." The city was her place. She'd never doubted that. Even after Ethan had unceremoniously told her their marriage was over... on the second day of their honeymoon. That still infuriated her. He'd known before their wedding that he hadn't wanted to go through with it, but he'd still stood at the altar and made vows he'd had no intention of keeping. And Bryn had been so focused on trying to make him happy that she'd refused to see the signs.

At least getting dumped in such a way had cracked every rose-colored pair of glasses in her wardrobe.

When moving out of their home, he'd asked if she was moving away. She'd told him no. Though she hadn't elaborated, it wasn't his business. She'd left the hospital they'd worked at but not the city.

Luckily, Boston was large enough that she never ran into him.

The food arrived, and Bryn leaned over, inhaling the spice and savoring the moment. Then she took her first bite and sighed.

"I agree." Nick took another bite of the food. "You were right—this is delicious."

"Told you."

* * *

Bryn looked at her watch. Her plate was gone. She'd finished her drink, and it was nearly time to take Honey on her last walk of the night. Which meant she needed to say good-night to Nick Walker.

The problem was she didn't want to.

Conversation had been so easy. They'd talked of books and movies—Nick was a huge cinema buff. The night was simple, and for the first time in forever, she felt like someone heard her.

If this had been a date, it would have gone down as the best first date of her life. And it was so relaxed, probably precisely because it wasn't a date.

Maybe she had a small crush on the hot new doc, but that didn't mean the feeling was mutual. They were two colleagues who had run into each other and had an enjoyable time. No need to read anything more into the situation.

"You keep looking at your watch."

Her cheeks heated as she met his supple brown eyes again. "I need to get Honey out for her night-time walk. If Abbie was in town, I could text her, but she switched places with Ailani for three months. A nurse rotation with our sister hospital in Hawaii. Abbie won't have a white Christmas, but maybe she'll get sand in her toes." And now she was rambling.

Get it together, Bryn!

"I just don't think it would be fair to ask Ailani to do it. It was her first day today. She's been in town a week, still settling and all." She motioned for Bill.

"Ready for the check?"

"Yes, please."

Bill looked at Nick, then back at her. "Separate?"

"Yes." Her face was hot. This was not a date. That the bartender even suspected…

"We work together." Bryn's voice was rugged, and she tilted her head toward Nick. "Just colleagues." Why was she expanding on this? All she needed to say was yes. She pursed her lips, forcing herself to stop talking.

"Got it." Bill's eyebrows pushed together as he turned to her companion. "You ready for the check?"

"Seems that way." Nick leaned against the bar as he pulled his wallet from his back pocket.

"Sorry. I…"

"What are you apologizing for?" Nick raised an eyebrow, his whole body was relaxed, and if one snapped a picture, they'd capture the image of the most handsome man in the place.

"I'm not sure." She shook her head. "I need to take Honey out."

"You do. She's an integral part of Ward 34."

Such a simple statement. One that if she hadn't already had a sizable crush on the man would have created one. Ethan hadn't supported her choice to train Honey as a therapy dog. He'd said animals had no place in medicine—despite so many studies refuting such nonsense.

He'd gifted her the puppy. Looking back at it, though, Bryn wondered if that was because people liked golden retrievers. Honey looked great in pictures; he could talk about the sweet dog at home. But he'd never cared for her, never snuggled with her. To him, Honey was just an animal.

To Bryn, the dog was her universe.

"From telling me dogs aren't allowed in the ward to 'an integral part' of the team. Quite the turnaround." She playfully pushed against his shoulder, and fire lit through her body. For a woman who'd just loudly proclaimed this wasn't a date, she couldn't seem to convince her body.

"I didn't realize she was a therapy dog." Nick winked as he stood and grabbed his coat. "Sometime you'll have to tell me how you trained her. I've met a few therapy dogs but never asked many questions."

Bryn stood, accepting Nick's offer when he grabbed her coat and held it open for her.

Not a date...

"The training center is right around the corner. Honey and I are teaching tomorrow morning—nine to eleven—before doing an afternoon shift at the hospital. I always grab a coffee at the Full of Beans Coffee shop at eight thirty, then walk…" She cleared her throat—he didn't need a rundown of her morning plans. "If you'd like to join us, you're welcome to."

"I just might do that."

Bryn knew her smile was gigantic. She also knew that "might do that" was not *see you tomorrow*. Still, he seemed serious.

"Thank you, Bryn."

"For what?"

"Spending the night with me." He walked with her to the door. "It was nice not to eat alone."

It was. "Good night, Nick." Bryn looked at her feet, then made herself walk away. She reached the corner and couldn't stop herself from looking back.

She turned her head and saw Nick. Just watching after her. The light of the restaurant pooled on his face. He looked like a mythical being…an Adonis. And all his attention was focused on her.

He raised a hand; she did the same. Then he turned and walked the other way. Bryn shook her head and hurried home. It was already almost thirty minutes past Honey's walk time… At least her puppy was the forgiving type. Because Bryn wouldn't change a thing about tonight.

It was easy to spot Bryn in the coffee shop. All Nick had to do was look for the gathering of children and hear the exclamations of "puppy" and

"Honey." Honey and Bryn must've been favorite regulars.

And why wouldn't they be?

Dogs were nearly universally loved, and Honey was a star. So was her handler.

And that was the reason he was coming into the coffee shop hours before his afternoon shift. Last night's dinner had been blissful. One of the best first nights out in his long history of new places.

He hadn't lied to Bryn, though he hadn't been exactly honest, either. Nick had walked up to the restaurant to look at the menu because it was busy. He might have eaten there. The menu looked good, and there was a crowd—always a good sign. But he'd seen Bryn taking off her coat and sitting at the bar.

Nick hadn't been able to open the door fast enough. He'd wanted to say hi. Wanted to eat with her. Wanted to spend time with her. It was a feeling so out of character. Nick moved on. It was his go-to.

The one constant in his ever-rotating location game.

His sister, Lisa, had once asked if he was chasing something. She'd been waiting to hear if she'd made Command. In that moment, she'd said she was looking forward to settling down. Finding some place warm year-round, her own home, maybe near a beach. Her eyes had held a sense of envy and judgment. Nick was the one not beholden to military orders. He was the one who could choose to stay.

And he never stayed.

Their father had walked in before Nick could answer. Holding the list of names for Command that Nick had known had contained his sister's. One perk of being the kid of the chairman of the joint chiefs—maybe the only one.

Lisa had bounded to their father, all hope for a different life fading as she'd heard that she'd made it. Commander of some center in Dayton, Ohio. Nowhere near a beach—and certainly not forever warm. In that moment, their father had looked so proud of her, and that was what mattered in the Walker house.

A look he never got.

Lisa had forgotten her question. But Nick hadn't. He wasn't looking for something—at least he didn't think so. Still, as Bryn looked up from her table, her eyes locking with his, he wondered if maybe staying in Boston longer was a good idea.

"Nick." Bryn's smile could light up a room. She wore a green sweater with a white snowman, matching Honey's snowman outfit. The two of them screamed Christmas.

"You look festive."

Bryn's smile faltered as she rubbed Honey's ears. "The kids love it."

"You don't?" She looked like she'd stepped out of a holiday catalogue. He wasn't an overly festive person. Decorations, holiday songs, bakery items sold in family-size packs with trees and wreath icing…they were fine.

There were people who lived for this time of year. Nick didn't mind it, but he didn't get excited about the shift from Halloween to Christmas. The trees and lights were pretty, but that was all.

However, if you had Christmas sweaters, surely that meant you loved the holiday.

Bryn ran her hand over the snowman, then looked at her phone. "We better get going. You ready?"

Nick held up his coffee. "Lead the way." She hadn't answered the Christmas question. Clearly a sore subject. That was a fact Nick understood.

People often asked why he volunteered for the holiday shifts. Why he never mentioned family. Why he moved all the time. There were no simple answers to those questions, and he was always grateful when people didn't push.

So he would let it go…but that didn't mean he didn't want to know.

They walked the couple of blocks to the therapy center in silence. It wasn't uncomfortable, though he wouldn't mind chatting with her more.

"Here we are." Bryn raised a hand, and Honey danced in front of a brightly colored door.

"So, is it okay if I sit in? I don't want to interrupt therapy. And I should have thought of that before just now." He'd been so focused on time with Bryn, on exploring something new with the beauty before him. As a doctor, he should have considered the implications of just dropping in on therapy.

Bryn shook her head. "This is the training center. People don't come here for therapy—we train the animals here. Then the handlers take the animals to the hospital, retirement center, schools, even workplaces."

"Animals?" He'd seen dogs in the hospital but nothing else. "More than dogs?"

"Yep." Bryn opened the door and motioned for Honey to stay while Nick walked in first. "Dogs are most common. But other animals go through training, too. We have a few cats, a rabbit, even a miniature horse."

"A horse!" The child in him wanted to scream with excitement. As a kid, he'd begged for riding lessons. The family had moved too much for that to become a reality. Still, there was something about the majestic beasts that called to him.

Bryn laughed. "Nick, does a mini horse excite you?"

"Who wouldn't be excited by that!"

"I hate to disappoint you, but Oreo, the mini horse, isn't scheduled for today."

"Ah." Nick shrugged as the excitement tapered off. "That's too bad. I'll have to tag along again when he's here." He shut his mouth. He'd just invited himself along… It was kind of Bryn to offer this visit once. For him to suggest—

"You're welcome anytime, Nick."

Pink coated her cheeks, and her soft smile sent heat straight to his heart. The world seemed to slow as her green eyes held his. His chest tightened as his breath caught.

"Bryn!" The call from the across the room broke the spell connecting them.

He could breathe easier…but he almost didn't want to. He wanted to know what the color meant in her cheeks. If she felt the connection between them, too.

"You brought a friend."

"Um." Bryn pushed a loose hair behind her ear as she looked over at Nick. "Yeah, a friend. And colleague. This is Dr. Nick Walker, the new pediatrician at Beacon Hospital. Honey's interaction with the kids fascinated him yesterday, and he wanted to see how we do things here. Though he's upset to miss Oreo."

"Oreo is only here on Mondays. He is a very busy horse." The middle-aged white woman held out her hand. "I'm Molly Anders, the director here."

"Nice to meet you." Nick gripped her hand. "I appreciate you letting me observe."

"Observe?" Molly shook her head, then looked

at Bryn. "Wes, our volunteer, is sick, and you're here. So how about you help us train?"

Nick knew his eyes were wide. He'd planned to sit in the back, watch, learn what he could, but taking part? He didn't know the first thing about animals—let alone working animals.

"I've never had a pet." He'd asked. So many times, but the answer from the general had always been no. And an order from the general, whether directed at subordinates or family, was always followed.

"Not a requirement." Bryn winked as she waved to a woman passing them with an animal in a carrier. "In fact, it's good to have a range of animal expertise because the patients will, too."

Molly nodded as she pointed toward a bright blue door. "I swear it's really not that bad. You can be Bryn and Honey's partner."

Bryn opened the door, motioned for Honey to wait and then grinned at him. "I promise to go easy with you."

He wanted to laugh, make some cute comment. Instead, his tongue stayed rooted to the top of his mouth.

Stepping into the room, he looked at the six dogs, all sitting nicely on the floor. One was another golden retriever, but the other five looked to be mutts varying from lap dog to a hundred-pound fella who looked up at him, his tail whapping against the floor.

"So what exactly is the plan?" Nick didn't mind being helpful, but his therapy dog experience was primarily limited to Honey's unorthodox introduction.

"You're going to be the patient. We'll run Honey through the drills, and then the other dogs will follow. You just need to sit and walk as directed. Think of yourself as an actor...with furry friends."

"Sorry! Sorry!" A young man raced past Nick and slid into the chair next to the giant dog, a medium gray-and-white dog bouncing behind him. "The bus is running late, and I just..." He shook his head and let out a sigh.

"Good morning, Adam." Bryn put a smile on her face. "It's nice to see you and Pepper. Please instruct her to sit."

He motioned with his hand, and the dog did nothing. "We're just a little hyped from the run in here." He motioned again and added, "Sit." Pepper ignored the instruction until he performed the same task a third time.

Adam scratched the top of the dog's head, then let out a clear sigh of relief.

Nick noticed a few of the other pet handlers didn't try to hide their frustration, but Bryn seemed unfazed by the issue. "Everyone, this is Nick Walker—our volunteer for the day."

The crowd clapped as Nick waved. Once more,

Pepper popped up but sat again as soon as instructed. At least she was listening now.

"All right, Nick, you ready?" Bryn and Honey stood next to him, waited for him to nod, then started walking through the drills. Honey's tail wagged the entire time, and Bryn smiled at him several times.

There were far worse ways to spend the hours before a shift.

"Biscuit's turn." The gentle giant Nick had noticed when he'd first walked in stood with his handler and started going through the same drills he'd done with Honey, Scout and three other dogs. Laying his head in Nick's lap, accepting pets on the head, gentle tugs on the ear. Listening to the commands that his owner, Rachel, gave, before Nick followed, too. Finally, it was time for the last move: Biscuit walking beside Nick as they moved through a recreated playroom. Toys, bells and claps echoed all around.

"You're doing great. I owe you for this," Bryn whispered as he rounded the corner.

"Maybe you do." He winked. He wasn't sure how he'd ask for repayment, but if she wanted to buy him a coffee…or let him buy her one, he wouldn't turn the opportunity down.

"Nice work, Biscuit."

No sooner had the words left Nick's mouth than he felt something brush up behind him, and then the world seemed to shift as Biscuit's back legs pushed against his own. Shifting, trying to regain balance, he heard a yelp and pulled his foot up as Pepper darted between his legs.

The floor rose to meet him. Nick put out his hands to catch himself, a reaction he knew was wrong but couldn't stop in the moment. He blew out a breath as pain shot up from his left wrist upon landing.

"Nick, are you all right?" Bryn was at his level, her blue eyes searching his face before reaching for his wrist. "Can you move it?"

Pepper danced beside him, and Nick moved the fingers in his hand. It was sore but not broken.

"Good motion in the fingers." Bryn's hand was warm on his. If his hand wasn't aching, Nick would enjoy this.

"Now…" Bryn let go of his hand. "Can you rotate it? Don't force it."

"I am a doctor, Bryn."

"I know. And doctors make the worst patients."

The phrase echoed in his mind as he gingerly rotated his wrist. It was a line he'd heard from more than one nurse. Unfortunately, they weren't wrong. Doctors made terrible patients.

"That a quip you picked up being a therapy-dog handler?"

Her cheeks coated with color as she watched him move his hand. "Let's focus on your wrist."

Another question deflected…

"Sore but nothing too bad. Tomorrow it will probably ache, but it's not broken."

"But it could have been." Molly crossed her arms and looked at Pepper's owner. "Adam, can I speak with you, please?"

Molly, Adam and Pepper headed out of the room, Pepper clearly oblivious to the hanging head of her owner.

Bryn clapped her hands. "Thanks, everyone. See you next weekend."

"Bryn." Nick stood, dusting himself off. "I hope I didn't get Pepper in trouble."

She frowned, and his heart dropped. "It was an accident, Bryn."

"I know. But it wasn't your fault, it was Pepper's." Bryn dropped Honey's leash, and he dog stayed right by her side. After a quick motion with her hand, Honey sat. Another motion, and Honey lay down.

"That was impressive."

"Not really. *Stay*, *sit*, *lie down* are all basic commands for dogs. I trained Honey with words and motions in case I have situations where words aren't ideal. Those are the basics." Bryn looked toward the door. "Pepper is a wonderful dog…"

Nick heard the mental *but* she wasn't saying. "But she won't be a therapy dog?" He rubbed the back of his head. "I'm not a regular volunteer. She just got excited."

"Exactly." Bryn nodded. "You are not a regular. You're new and exciting."

"Right." Nick looked at the door again. The sweet dog and their owner had not returned.

"You're also tall, young, strong—"

"Are you trying to woo me?"

Woo? He'd landed on his hand, not his head. Still, the hint of pink brightening in Bryn's cheeks made him happier than he'd been in forever.

She cleared her throat. "The patients won't all be as fit or young as you are. They'll also be new and, if Pepper goes to a school, young and jumpy. So…" Bryn snapped her fingers in a quick pattern.

Honey grabbed her leash in her mouth and handed it to her.

"So Pepper isn't a good fit." He knew dogs failed at service training. Not every animal was meant to work, but…

"Sorry you were the last test. Not intentional, but I know it sucks."

"*Sucks.* That is a good word for it."

Bryn looked at her watch, then back at Nick. "Honey and I are in the ER this afternoon. Want to walk to the hospital together?"

"Absolutely."

CHAPTER THREE

"I DON'T KNOW what I expected of Boston in the winter, but walking through the park and seeing kids and families playing wasn't it."

Bryn laughed and pointed to the sky. "The sun is shining. It's not *too* chilly. You've lived so many places—you've really never experienced kids playing outside in December?"

"I have." Nick chuckled as a child raced across the path in front of them. "I guess I just figured there'd be more snow!"

"This is Boston. Not Maine."

Nick opened his mouth, but before he could deliver a witty statement, a scream echoed from the playground they'd just passed. He took off without thinking.

He turned and noticed Bryn and Honey keeping pace with him.

Reaching the playground, Nick could see a young boy between seven and nine on the ground. Blood coated the side of his head, and the boy didn't seem conscious.

A woman was kneeling beside him, tears streaming across her face. "Isaac. Isaac. Isaac."

"Stay."

He heard Bryn issue the command to Honey as he stepped toward the boy. "I'm a doctor."

"Call 911," Bryn stated behind her. "Tell them a doctor and nurse are on site but that we need emergency transport for a child."

"Nurse?" Nick raised a brow as she kneeled beside him. There wasn't time to discuss that, but when this was over...

Bryn put her fingers on the boy's wrist. "Pulse is rapid but strong."

That was a good sign.

"His breathing is consistent." Nick wanted the boy to open his eyes, but as far as he and Bryn could tell, the child was stable.

"His right arm is under him awkwardly, there's a cut above his eyebrow and, based on the surrounding blood, at least one on the back of his head, and..." Bryn looked at Nick, and he nodded.

The child had fallen. Potential neck injuries did not get moved without stabilization unless absolutely necessary. The cut was bleeding, adding to the blood on the child's face, but head wounds bled. It was possible it just needed a few stitches and looked nastier than it was.

"What happened?" Nick looked at the woman crying.

She hiccupped and said something, but it was unintelligible through the sobs.

Bryn motioned with her hand, and Honey moved beside the woman, pressing her body to her.

"Ma'am, I need you to take a deep breath." Her words were soft but direct. "Isaac is bleeding and unconscious. Can you tell Dr. Walker what happened?"

"He was doing tricks." The words came from behind him.

He turned to find a small girl—not the ideal firsthand witness, but he'd take anything.

"Tricks." Nick nodded. "Did he fall after the trick?"

She looked at Isaac, then back at Nick. "He was flipping. I told him I wanted a turn, and he looked at me weird. I told him to stop it. Then he dropped."

Looked at me weird…that could be anything from he'd made a face to rapid eye movement indicating something far more serious.

"Does your son have a history of seizures?" Bryn's words were firm. Clearly her mind had gone to where his had traveled, too. "We need to tell the paramedics."

"No." His mother fumbled for a tissue. "No, Isaac has always been healthy."

No history of seizures. That didn't mean much. Seizures weren't as common as television drama made them seem, and their causes were far vaster than the average person realized.

"His father was epileptic." The woman sucked in a deep breath. "It was well controlled, but then one night…" She blew out a breath and leaned against Honey.

He looked at Bryn and saw her bite her lip. Epilepsy was a difficult diagnosis. Even when the condition was well controlled, it was possible for the worst to happen. And Isaac's mom didn't have to finish the sentence for the medical professionals to know what she couldn't voice.

There was no way to diagnose it in the field, but the one bright point was that while epilepsy could begin at any age, its onset in childhood was unusual. It was family history the paramedics needed to know, but it didn't mean Isaac had had his first epileptic seizure.

"I hear the sirens." Bryn's shoulders relaxed.

She must've been feeling the same relief he was. There was little they could do for Isaac outside of assessing stability and getting frontline questions answered.

"Mom." The boy's eyes fluttered open, and he shifted.

"Stay still." Bryn laid a hand on Isaac's chest. Not pushing him down, but letting him know people were there. Head trauma often resulted in patients trying to get up and move. Some scientists believed it was an evolutionary leftover, the body going into flight mode. *Something injured me—must move.*

Nick wasn't sure, but he'd seen enough people and children follow the pattern to know Bryn's choice was a good one.

"Mom," Isaac repeated.

"I'm here." The boy's mother leaned over and kissed one of the few places free of blood. "I'm right here. But the nurse is right—you must stay still."

"What happened?" Isaac's voice was quiet with a thready, almost dreamlike quality to it.

"We're not sure," Nick stated. He and Bryn didn't have any answers.

"My head hurts."

"I bet it does." She smiled at the boy. "Can you hear the ambulance sirens?"

"Yeah."

"Well, they're going to take you to the hospital. You've got a cut on your forehead and at least one cut on the back of your head, too." Bryn looked up at his mom and then back at the boy. "You will probably have stitches."

Isaac moved his hand, but Nick caught it. "I know this is confusing, but I need you to stay as still as possible until the medics get here."

"Am I going to be all right?" The child's bottom lip trembled. "My dad."

"You aren't your dad." His mother broke in. "You're going to be fine. Perfectly fine."

Bryn snapped her fingers, and Honey moved from Isaac's mother's side and lay down next to him.

"She's pretty." He raised a hand and ran it along the dog's head.

"She is beautiful. And she knows it." Bryn used a mock high-pitched voice as she winked at Honey.

"I like her sweater." Isaac's voice was low. That was good. Adrenaline and stress were natural responses to trauma but not healing.

There was no way to know what exactly had occurred, but it was clear that Isaac and his mother were thinking of his dad. Worrying— which was understandable. And once more, Honey was here to offer a fuzzy ear.

"It's one of her favorites." Bryn flicked the headband the dog was wearing, causing the bells to ring.

"It matches your sweater."

"It does." Her voice wavered a little. Then she moved her hand to the sweater, pushed an unseen button and it lit up.

"Whoa!" Isaac's words were soft, filled with wonder. "It's so pretty."

Nick looked at their patient: Isaac's coloring was good. He was calm—mostly. There was more blood than Nick would like, but it wasn't gushing.

He looked over Bryn's shoulder. The sirens

were getting closer, and he could see the ambulance coming through the park entrance.

Rationally, Nick knew it had only been a few minutes, fifteen minutes top, since the emergency call had gone out. But when a child was injured, time simultaneously sped up and slowed down.

"All right, the paramedics are here, Isaac." Nick shifted so Isaac could look at him and keep petting Honey without moving.

"When they get over here, they are going to put something around your neck. It will make sure that you can't move, and it can feel scary. It's necessary to keep you safe."

"They used it on my dad once when he had a seizure and fell." Isaac's bottom lip trembled, and he squeezed his eyes shut. "I can do this."

"You can." His mother kissed him again. "I will be right with you."

The first paramedic ran up, and Bryn stepped back and the lights on her sweater flipped off. She motioned for Honey to follow her and waved to Isaac.

The boy lifted a hand but stayed still.

Nick stood and quickly filled in the second paramedic on what they'd learned and observed. And in just a few minutes, Isaac was on the backboard and loaded into the ambulance.

He stood by Bryn as the ambulance pulled away. "So, you're a registered nurse?"

* * *

"Yes." Bryn started to cross her arms, then stopped herself. Beacon had hired her as a therapy-dog handler, but Javier knew she was an RN. He'd mentioned twice to her that Ward 34 needed nurses, that they could put her on the floor the second she was ready to slide back into her scrubs.

She'd considered it on more than one occasion when she'd been lying awake late at night. The urge to try it, to change the quiet pattern she'd slipped into pulling at her. But she hadn't taken that step.

"But now you aren't?" Nick's hands were in his pockets, his eyes trained on the departing vehicle.

She could tell from his stance that he wouldn't push her. And that upset her. Which made little sense. Part of the reason she was so happy that Abbie was in Hawaii was because that meant no one knew why Bryn had left nursing. Why she was spending Christmas alone with her dog. Why she was avoiding the magical things she normally so looked forward to.

"My ex-husband is a pediatric orthopedic surgeon at Brigham." The sentence flew from her mouth, and she had to fight the urge to hang her head. That Ethan had called an end to their union just after stepping off the plane on their honeymoon wasn't her fault. But how had she not seen that the man standing opposite from her at the altar had had no interest in getting, let alone staying, married?

How had she let herself change so much for him?

"I see."

"Really?" Even Bryn didn't fully understand her choice.

"No." Nick shrugged. "Lots of people get divorced and continue working in the field they were in before they got married."

"How many of them work with colleagues who danced at their wedding on Saturday and learned by Friday that the husband had already called it quits?"

Nick's eyes widened, but he had the good grace not to say anything.

"Everyone—and I mean everyone—at that wedding worked with us. My mom passed a few years ago. Ethan's parents aren't in the picture. He said it was because they didn't support him—not sure if anything he said was true. I just…"

Bryn swallowed the lump in her throat. She'd not voiced any of this in a year.

Because everyone I know knows this sob story.

"We got married the week before Christmas… and filed for divorce before New Year's. Before all the holiday decorations were even put away! You don't get a break on lawyers' fees based on the length of your union."

"That seems decidedly unfair."

"Thank you." Bryn pushed the button at the crosswalk and pulled her coat around her as the wind picked up.

Nick stepped forward. Not much, but enough to offer a windbreak. "I'm surprised you don't hate Christmas."

"I do." That wasn't exactly true, but the holiday had certainly lost more than a bit of its sparkle. Though Ethan had contributed to that, too. He hated fun decor. Hated homemade cookies. Pretty much all the things she loved.

"Bryn, that isn't true."

She put her hands on her hips and stared up at him, something that might've been intimidating if her heart didn't pick up as his cool brown eyes met hers. "You've known me for days, *Dr. Walker*. I think I know what I like about this season and what I don't."

Nick looked down at Honey…then flicked the antlers on the top of the golden retriever's head. "Your dog is in a holiday sweater, wearing antlers."

"She's a therapy dog."

"And you're in a matching sweater."

Heat flooded her cheeks, but she didn't look down at the snowman sweater. The bright, obnoxious snowman sweater that she'd flung on this morning without thinking. "It matches Honey."

"Yes. And it lights up, Bryn. No one who hates Christmas has a light-up snowman sweater."

The light changed before she could think of a retort. They hustled across the street as horns blared. They had the right of way, but that didn't mean the Boston drivers cared to give it.

"I took a break." The sentence was soft, but it echoed in her heart. A break. That was what this year was. A break from dating. A break from nursing. A break from holidays and celebrations.

"*Took* is past tense." Nick stopped as Beacon Hospital's entrance came into view.

"A figure of speech."

"Look me in the eye and tell me you don't miss nursing."

She couldn't do that. Bryn loved working with Honey. Loved seeing patients' faces light up when the dog walked into the room. But it wasn't the same as providing day-to-day care.

"You're signed up for the Santa Dash, the bake sale—"

"I know, but all that is for the kids. And to raise money for Camp Heartlight." The words sounded slightly hollow even to her. "The last year… I just… I just…"

"Put yourself in hibernation?" Nick's question hit her in the chest.

Hibernation. She rolled the word around her subconscious. The descriptor was accurate. She didn't miss Ethan. He was a jerk, something she should have realized before she'd been standing in white before all their friends.

Their friends.

His friends. Or rather, colleagues who thought his meteoric rise in pediatric surgery might help their careers—if he liked them. Not realizing that Ethan only liked one person.

Himself.

But she'd lost herself in that moment. Lost the free spirit that believed people were generally good. Yes, there were bad people. Her father was a disappointment, but after growing up without him, Bryn had thought she could spot the users.

Ethan walking away—on their honeymoon—had shaken her to her core.

"Hibernation is safe."

"And lonely." Nick rocked back on heels as he looked up at the building. "I've started over more than a dozen times in my life. Hibernation is a defense mechanism. Don't let it steal something you love."

"You sound like Javi." Bryn laughed. "He's eager for me to get back on the floor."

"A nurse quit a few days ago. It's got him worried. And he has a therapy-dog handler already through the hospital background checks, already employed by the hospital part time, who is a registered nurse. I'm stunned he's not following you around every time you walk onto the ward."

"That's not Javi's style." Bryn liked the head of Pediatrics. He was quiet, but he cared about his staff. Which was considerably more than she could say for her ex.

"What if we make a deal?"

"A deal?" Why did she say that? She should have said no. There was no reason to bring herself out of hibernation, as Nick had called it. She was safe.

Her world was small, but it was safe.

Still…

"I help you come out of hibernation, and you show me around Boston. The fun stuff. The touristy stuff and the hidey holes only the locals know about."

"And step one is talking to Javi about picking up nursing shifts?" Bryn's heart raced as she stepped through the entrance. She could start as soon as she wanted. If she wanted…

And Nick was right—she wanted to.

CHAPTER FOUR

NICK'S CELL BUZZED, and he reached over his couch to grab it. He couldn't stop the smile as he saw Bryn's name pop onto the screen.

Javi talked to HR. I start Friday.

It didn't surprise him Javi had talked to HR on Bryn's behalf. If the floor wasn't fully staffed, that meant that they couldn't admit as many patients. While the pediatric ward was never quiet, the winter months were very full. With people inside, children sharing germs at school and extracurriculars, influenza, RSV and other childhood illnesses cropped up more frequently.

For most children, this meant a few days off school, their parents making sure they drank enough fluids and took naps, but for some, it meant hospitalization.

That is fantastic. I can't wait to work with you!

As Nick typed back, his mind was already shifting to the other parts of this plan. Helping Bryn step back into nursing was the first step in pulling her out of her hibernation.

Why do I care so much?

That was a question that had rumbled around his brain for days. Nick was always polite to his colleagues. He considered a few of them friends, but he didn't get close. In any other situation, he might have suggested to a nurse or doctor that they return to the field, but he wouldn't have pushed.

Wouldn't have cut a deal with them.

I owe you some real Boston insights now. Want to grab dinner? Pizza?

Yes. He wanted to do that so bad. But he'd put off unpacking his apartment for weeks. Living in boxes was something he didn't mind. Hell, when he'd been in Atlanta, he'd not bothered to unpack half his stuff. It had just made it easier when he'd picked up and headed out again.

But the boxes had bothered him for days now. Since he'd met Bryn. Because inviting someone over while the only things unpacked were a week's worth of clothes and his movie collection was something he wouldn't do. And he wanted to invite Bryn over. Wanted to cook dinner and watch movies. As friends...

There was no point in lying. He was attracted to the woman. How could he not be? She was sunshine in a bottle, with light blond hair always pulled into some fancy braid, bright green eyes and a smile that seemed to push against his heart every time he saw it. However, you could be friends with someone you found attractive. And that was what he was going to be—friends with Bryn.

I want to say yes, but I finally started unpacking my apartment. If I stop now I might never start again.

At least he knew himself. If Nick didn't unpack the boxes, then he wouldn't invite Bryn over. So that meant this needed to be done.

Want help?

Two words on the screen. Two words that made his soul leap.

Yes.

He'd typed it and hit Send before he could think Bryn's offer through.

Then I need an address.

The smile emoji at the end of the sentence made him laugh. No one in his family used emojis in texts. His father had forbidden them years ago. Nick had never understood why the general hated them, but the family had followed the order.

He typed out his address, hit Send and sighed as she told him she'd see him in thirty minutes.

The knock at his door almost exactly thirty minutes later sent a lightning bolt through every nerve in Nick's body. Bryn was here. To help him unpack a life he never fully unboxed. His feet rushed across the apartment like they couldn't reach the door soon enough.

She was wearing dark yoga pants, a plain pink sweatshirt and she'd pulled her hair into a messy bun that sat on the top of her head. In short, she was breathtaking.

Man, he really had it bad.

"Bryn Bedford, reporting for duty." She made a fake salute, then giggled. "How was my salute?"

"As good as my *wicked*." He winked as she stepped into the apartment.

"Ouch!" She playfully made a motion with her hand over her heart like she was pulling a knife from her chest. "Wow, you weren't kidding. This place isn't unpacked."

"Why would I lie?"

"I…" Her cheeks darkened as she looked toward the kitchen.

Had she been hoping he was looking for an excuse to invite her over? He was glad she was here, and if she wanted to just pop in a movie and chill, well, he wouldn't argue.

"Where do you want to start, Nick?"

"Kitchen? It's past time I stopped getting take-out to avoid doing dishes."

Laughing, Bryn moved toward the open kitchen. Then she stopped as she hit the living room, and he nearly ran into her.

"How many movies do you have?"

Her eyes were staring at the long wall in the living room, just opposite his kitchen. It was full of movies, from the baseboards to the ceiling. And those were only the ones he'd kept. Most of his library was on streaming services now. But these, well, these had come with him from place to place for too long to give away.

"I guess that number depends on if you're talking about just these or the online library, too. Though most of those I own on streaming, too. It's my hobby." Nick pulled at the back of his neck. Movies and film were his passion.

In a dark theater with the characters on-screen, a big fresh container of popcorn. It had been the perfect way for a lonely kid to lose a few hours.

"Do you like movies?" It was usually one of the first questions he asked on a date. Though this wasn't a date.

In fact, it felt much more intimate.

"Not as much as you." She smiled and walked to the wall. "You have everything here. Romance, horror, documentary, foreign…"

"Yeah. I don't really have a favorite genre. I just watch anything."

"What's your favorite?" Her eyes were bright as she turned to look at him.

"Favorite?" Nick let out a breath as he looked at the wall. "I don't think there's any way for me to choose. Almost every film has something I like about it. The story or the characters or the score. I mean…"

"I like holiday films. Or I did. I used to start watching them as soon as the turkey from Thanksgiving was put away. Ethan, my ex, wasn't a huge fan." Bryn let out a chuckle. "He wasn't a huge fan of anything. Funny how easy it is to see that now."

She clapped her hands, clearly trying to move past the words she'd said. "Unpack the kitchen. That's our goal tonight."

"It is." Nick grinned as he followed her into the kitchen. He didn't mind the statements about her ex. In fact, he enjoyed hearing them. Which was weird because that shouldn't have been the case. But he suspected Bryn hadn't talked about her ex in a while. Maybe since he'd decided their short-lived marriage wouldn't work.

Her talking about it with Nick meant she trusted him with the knowledge.

Or she's figured out I'm safe because I don't stay.

Nick wanted to pull that thought from his mind. No reason to seek the worst thoughts. Bryn was sharing with him. That was nice—no matter the circumstances. "Want me to put one on while we unpack? I've probably got any holiday movie you can think of."

Bryn put a hand on her chin, her eyes glowing. "That is such a challenge. What movie could I think of that you don't have?"

He crossed his arms, knowing his smile was gigantic. This was the perfect kind of challenge for him. With a woman who heated his blood and made him happy. A friend. Bryn was a friend.

Something he shouldn't have to keep reminding himself of.

"Come up with something?"

"No." She tapped her head again, then shrugged. "All I can think of is *Miracle on 34th Street*. And that's the exact opposite of obscure."

"It is." He winked, picked up the remote he kept on the kitchen counter, turned on the television and quickly found the classic in his online stash.

"*Miracle on 34th Street* and unpacking. Not a bad way to spend the night."

Nick nodded. "Not a bad way at all, Bryn."

* * *

"Pizza should be here in about twenty minutes." Nick slid into the doorway by his study. His dark shirt had packing dust on it, but it couldn't diminish the beauty of the man.

Bryn!

She still couldn't believe she'd asked if he'd wanted help unpacking. Most women would have taken it as a blow off when they'd invited a man to dinner.

Not exactly *I'm washing my hair*, but close enough.

But she'd felt deep inside that he hadn't been lying to her. Hadn't been looking for an excuse. So she'd offered help, mostly expecting another rejection.

Part of her had kind of hoped for it. Nick was sweet, kind, intelligent and drop-dead gorgeous. And her colleague. Particularly since she was starting rounds on the pediatric floor this Friday.

He was off-limits.

If only her libido could get on the same page as her brain.

"Good—I'm famished." And she needed some kind of distraction. Though eating with Nick likely wouldn't diminish the blooming crush she had on the doctor.

She cut open the last box from the closet. It was full of coins, books and memorabilia from West Point.

His father had been in the army. So were his siblings. Was he storing stuff for them?

"Where do you want this stuff?" She held up an Army field manual.

"Oh…umm, nowhere. Just leave it in the box." Nick's cheek twitched as his jaw locked down, his easy-going stance shifting.

"Is this your father's stuff?" Bryn placed the field manual back in the box and closed it up.

"No." Nick pressed his hands together and cleared his throat. "I think that just about does it. Thanks for the help. Pizza. Pizza should be here soon."

"Nick?" Bryn stepped close to him. He was stiff, his eyes focused on the space over her shoulder. "Nick."

She reached for his hand, hoping to ground him in the present. "Look at me." When he didn't follow her command, she squeezed again and stated, "Nick, look at me."

"It's no big deal."

"I didn't ask." Bryn pressed her free palm to his chest. "Why don't you get us something to drink while we wait for the pizza?"

"I have a red wine. It's a dry wine." Nick cleared his throat as he shook his head, then pulled his hand from hers. "Since we unpacked the kitchen, I know exactly where the wine glasses and bottle opener are."

He grinned, but his features didn't quite light up.

"Red works well with pizza." Bryn wasn't much a wine person. She enjoyed the drink, but she didn't know if people recommended red for pizza. It didn't matter. Whatever memories this box had awakened were moving away now that he had a new focus. That was what mattered.

"I'll go pour, and just put…umm…" His eyes wandered to the box on the office chair.

"Back in the closet?"

In the trash? If it caused him so much pain, she wasn't sure why he carted the box from place to place, but it was his and she'd do with it as he asked.

"Closet sounds great."

"All right, then." Bryn deposited the box, then went to the kitchen. Nick was standing at the kitchen counter, gripping it with his eyes tightly shut.

She moved without thinking, placing her arms around his waist and just holding him. His fingers left the counter and lay over hers at his waist. He didn't move, didn't speak, but that was all right.

How often after her marriage had ended had she just wanted to be held? It was a simple thing. A connection—reminding you that even though you were at a low point, the world still thought of you. You still mattered.

They stood like that for several minutes before Nick turned.

She dropped her hands. Her cheeks were burning. She'd just squeezed him, held him for minutes, and now she didn't know what to say.

"I owe you a glass of wine."

Bryn nodded, not quite trusting her voice.

He poured without saying anything, then passed her the glass.

"That was my West Point stuff." He took a deep sip.

"I thought you weren't in the military?" The wine was good, would go well with the pizza when it got here, but it could have been terrible, and it wouldn't matter. She was listening to Nick's story, one she was sure he rarely shared.

"I wasn't." Nick let out a long sigh. "I couldn't hack it. Not cut out for service."

Disappointment oozed off him, and she wanted to throttle whoever had told him that.

"So you started at West Point and left?"

"I finished my pleb year—the first year."

"Freshman year. That's the nonmilitary term for the first year."

Nick cracked a smile and his shoulders relaxed some. "Yeah. The army called us yuks second year—sophomore year. Short for *yearling*, but not sure anyone ever used that.

"Pleb year you go through Beast—it's a six-week basics class. And if your dad is a high-ranking military member…that does not buy you leniency. I made it through, was top of my class my first year, but I dreaded going back for yuk year. Still, I showed up…started Buckner, the three-week cadet field training. After I finished it, just before starting the academic year, I broke."

"Broke?" Bryn raised a brow. "What does that mean?"

"Just what it sounds like. I realized I couldn't do it. I couldn't stay. Couldn't graduate. The only one of my siblings to walk away from the uniform. My father hasn't looked at me the same since."

"You're a literal doctor." Bryn knew nervous laughter wasn't great, but her brain couldn't stop it. "Seriously, Nick. You're a doctor. A man who saves children's lives. That's not even overstating it—that is legit your job."

"He didn't even show for my med school graduation. I stood there all alone while everyone took pictures with their family. My field isn't good enough for the general."

"Well, that is just too damn bad." She set the wineglass on the counter. How dare his family ignore such a momentous occasion. If they walked up to her right now, she'd given them several pieces of her mind.

Nick's brown eyes caught and held hers. He pursed his lips, then set his wineglass down and started laughing. The rich sound growing deeper as the laugh grew stronger. "It sounds ridiculous, doesn't it?"

It sounded cruel, but she kept that thought

to herself. "I've seen you with patients, Nick. Watched kids, terrified children settle as you calm their—and their parents'—worries. You are exactly where you're meant to be."

"I could have gone to medical school after West Point. Served as an Army doctor."

"Would you have gotten to be a pediatrician?"

"I don't know. You serve at the needs of the armed forces when you go on their dime. If they needed pediatricians, then yes, if not..." He shrugged.

"If not, then you'd have gotten pushed into a specialty the army needed, right?"

"Yes."

"I think you were meant to be a pediatrician. So, it's a good thing you left when you did, but..." She paused, the question caught on the tip of her tongue.

"But?" Nick raised a brow. "Don't stop now. We've entered all new friendship territory here tonight."

Friendship. It was the right word. The word she wanted, too, but it struck her chest as she looked at him.

"But why keep a box that only brings you hurt?"

"I don't know." Nick finished his wine and poured a bit more into his glass. "My father wanted so badly for me to go, it felt wrong to throw it out."

"He didn't want you to be happy?" Why was that such a hard choice for some parents? Bryn saw loving parents all the time. But her mother had focused so much on her own happiness… tied to a man who wouldn't love her. And Nick's family wanted him to follow their path instead of their own.

Nick rolled his eyes. "Oh, he wanted us to be happy. Happy in the life he'd chosen."

"Was he happy?" The question popped out, and Bryn could tell by the snap of Nick's neck that he'd never considered the question.

"I…" He blinked over and over, like he was trying to funnel through a load of memories and coming up short. "I don't know."

A knock echoed through the apartment, and Bryn nearly jumped.

"That will be the pizza." Nick's body language shifted. The hurt son vanishing as he moved to answer the door. The confident doctor was back, the man secure in his place. But it was a shell, and deep inside was a hurt that she just wanted to wrap in a hug and force away.

Unfortunately, Bryn knew from experience that that was not how healing worked.

CHAPTER FIVE

BRYN YAWNED AS she walked up the steps to her apartment. Honey pressed her head against her legs, but she could tell the golden was tired, too. As the days got shorter, it was easy for her body to think that five was bedtime when the sun had set over an hour ago. Plus, she was putting in more hours with Paws for Hope since she was returning to nursing in three days. Three days to a new start.

Opening the apartment door, Bryn paused as Ailani waved…her hand full of the fake snow she was laying along the mantle of their faux fireplace. There was a small gas fire unit the landlord had sworn was a selling point.

A real fireplace, one with crackling wood… well, they existed, just not in apartment units in Bryn's price range.

Christmas decor. Usually by this time of year, her place looked like Santa had snapped his finger and turned it into a winter wonderland. She'd decorated her and Ethan's home every year… alone.

Bryn had sworn she wouldn't decorate this year. Sworn she was doing nothing. That her hibernation was keeping her safe.

The decorations were inexpensive, but they ignited a light in the dark room of her soul she was trying to ignore. Like Nick pointed out, she was wearing her sweaters. Dressing Honey is holiday cheer. Why keep herself from something she genuinely enjoyed?

"I hope you don't mind." Ailani's grin was wide as she held up a plain red stocking. "It's December, and it just felt like the apartment need a little cheer."

Bryn looked at the decorations and pursed her lips. Ailani was only in Boston for three months. She didn't deserve a Grinch for a roommate. "Do you want to decorate? I mean really, really decorate?"

Ailani's dark hair fell to the side as she tilted her head. "What does 'really, really decorate' mean?"

Bryn giggled. "It means let me put Honey in her crate because she needs a nap, then why don't you come with me to my storage unit in the basement? We can make this place glitter!"

She clapped and nodded. "Glitter! Yes. This place needs some holiday glitter."

* * *

"You weren't kidding." Ailani wiped her hand over her forehead as Bryn put the star on the Christmas tree they'd decorated in the corner. "This place looks like a winter wonderland. And there are still boxes in the storage unit."

Bryn sighed as she stepped off the step ladder. "My old place was a house. My ex-husband barely noticed the decorations and didn't ask for any of them when we split our stuff."

Which was good because she'd had no plans to let Ethan have her precious holiday decor.

"Some of it is really unique."

"Like what?" Bryn looked at the lights, the stockings. Ethan had had very distinct tastes regarding decor. Most of her fun stuff had stayed in boxes when they'd lived together. Seeing it all out tonight stitched a little piece of her soul.

"You have bean holiday lights."

"Oh." Bryn shook her head as she looked at the strand.

"I thought Bostonians hated the nickname Beantown."

"We do." It was a terrible nickname, one more than a few opinion articles had recommended discarding, but nicknames were not things that one could just throw away.

"So the bean lights…"

"Were from a white-elephant party a few years ago. My friend Indigo found them, thought they were hilarious. The party all vied for them—you know how sometimes the silliest gift is the one people want the most."

"But you won them?"

"Traded a set of shot glasses for them." Shot glasses Ethan had, apparently, wanted. Not bad enough to bring his own white-elephant gift, but somehow that had been her fault, too.

"I triumphed." The aftermath of that triumph had been terrible, but in the moment, when the bean lights were hers, she'd felt such a rush.

"This is the first year I've hung them up."

"I like them." Ailani grinned, then turned and headed to their small kitchen. "Before we take the empty boxes back to the storage unit, I feel like hot chocolate. What about you?"

"Hot chocolate after holiday decorating? It almost feels like a requirement."

Ailani made the drinks, passing Bryn one of the Santa mugs they'd dug out and hand-washed just an hour ago.

"There is something about hot chocolate…" Bryn sighed as she moved toward the sofa.

"It tastes better when it's cold, too." Ailani slid onto the other side of the couch. "Funny how hot coffee is a thing everywhere, but somehow drinking hot chocolate when it's around eighty degrees just isn't the same."

"True. I love hot cocoa this time of year, but by mid-March, the drink loses all interest for me. It's just this time of year, it's cozy and grounding." Bryn was excited for the changes coming. Mostly.

"You ready for Friday?" Ailani's dark eyes held Bryn's over her identical Santa mug.

"Yes. And no." Bryn shook her head, wishing there was some way to make the conflicting feelings make sense. "I want to go back, I do. I just—"

"You're nervous?"

"Yes, like I was my first day at Brigham years ago. I mean, I was a nurse for almost a decade when I stepped away. I shouldn't be nervous."

"Sure you should." Ailani's face held no malice, no mean intent, but she said the words with force.

"It feels like I shouldn't. Like I should just be thrilled. And I am thrilled. Part of my soul feels like dancing at the idea of putting my stethoscope back in my pocket."

"Adventure is like that. It's thrilling and makes your chest pound, but it's terrifying, too. The what-ifs, the worries that you might choose the wrong path."

"Says the woman who left her warm, sandy island to come to frozen Boston, where she doesn't know anyone."

"Yeah, and part of that was terrifying." Ailani sipped her hot chocolate. "Still wouldn't change a thing, though."

There was the hint of something in Ailani's eyes. A far-off hope that Bryn didn't think was tied to hot chocolate, Christmas decorations or travel.

"I'm excited to be working as a nurse." Bryn swallowed, then added, "And the new pediatrician, Nick…"

She got those words out, then her mouth refused to let any other pass.

"He's cute." Ailani winked. "And he promised if he heard of any good restaurants, he'd let me know. Newbies sticking together and all."

"If you want recommendations, I'm happy to give them." Technically, she'd promised Nick she'd take him around Boston. Show him the hidden and not-so-hidden gems of the city. She could invite Ailani.

That would put her and Nick's outings in strictly friend territory. Force her to ignore the pull her body had when she was in his presence. It was the easy answer.

So why am I not offering?

"Javi has given me some recommendations, too." A little color coated Ailani's tan cheeks, then she cleared her throat. "Ready to take the boxes down?"

Bryn set her Santa mug down and stood. She had questions about the color in the other woman's cheeks, but then Ailani probably had thoughts about her own statements about Nick.

And she didn't feel like sharing those, either.

* * *

Nick's lungs burned as he pulled in another breath of cold air. He privately swore at himself for signing up for the Santa Dash. He technically didn't need to train for the five-kilometer race fundraiser benefiting Camp Heartlight, and with each ragged breath he questioned just walking the race. But that meant even more time in the cold air.

It was an unfortunate reality that many children with chronic issues couldn't attend traditional summer camp. Camp Heartlight offered summer camp for children with chronic heart conditions. The staff for the two-week event were all nurses, doctors and paramedics. All trained to support the children if they had a medical emergency…but the camp was really about playing games, swimming, horseback riding and doing arts-and-crafts projects.

Nick had signed up as soon as he'd heard about the camp's mission. A five-kilometer race, starting in the park and ending with hot chocolate and doughnuts at the entrance of the hospital. No big deal…except it was December and his lungs had wanted to riot from moment his feet hit the pavement.

He knew the kids were planning to watch the race from the windows of the play area. And that was the only thing that kept his body moving as he pushed himself through the workout.

"Nick!" Bryn waved as she and Honey, dressed in outdoor running gear, passed him.

He'd known that she'd signed up for the Santa Dash, too. All right, maybe there were two reasons he was torturing himself in the frosty morning air.

He turned and headed toward Bryn and Honey.

She smiled as he came up beside them. Her nose was pink and her cheeks flushed, but the cold didn't seem to bother her as they kept pace together around the park.

When he thought his lungs might explode from the cold, he finally huffed, "How much longer you going?"

She sucked in a deep breath.

How did that not freeze her lungs?

"I have one more lap, then we go to Full of Beans for coffee, a blueberry muffin and a dog treat."

"Want some company?"

Her eyes glittered as they held his for just a moment before she focused on where she was putting her feet. A smart thought. "You are always welcome, Nick."

One more lap. He could do that. He could do anything if it meant more time with Bryn.

They ran the final steps in silence, and his body wanted to scream as Full of Beans came into view. Yes!

Bryn slowed, pulling up next to the shop. He

started for the door, but she stayed in place, pulling one leg up behind her while she held Honey's leash in her other hand. "You need to stretch before you go inside."

Nick looked at the warm shop, the smell of coffee pulling at his nose. "I mean, it's warm in there... I could get us coffee, and that way you and Honey don't have to wait."

"What is it about doctors and not taking care of themselves?"

"Spoken like a true nurse." Nick shook his head, then mimicked her movement. She was right. He needed to stretch, and heading from the cold to a shop that was likely forty degrees warmer would play hell on his muscles.

"Well, I'm headed back onto the nursing floor."

Her smile warmed the frozen parts of him. She looked so happy. Nursing was her calling. Working as a therapy-dog handler helped, but it wouldn't give her everything she needed.

"Ward 34 will be even more lovely with you there." The pediatric floor was wonderful, and it seemed to radiate holiday cheer. There was always some fancy sweet treat in the staff break room. The giant fake tree had ornaments made by the kids, the staff was kind. It was the best place he'd ever worked.

"Ready for coffee?"

"I thought you'd never ask!" Nick pulled the door open and waited for Bryn and Honey to step through. "Grab us a seat. I'll get the coffee and treats."

"Nick—"

"No arguing. I wouldn't have finished my training session without you guys. Go." He waved them away.

Bryn hesitated for a moment, then tugged on Honey's leash, heading for the booth in the back as Nick turned to place their order.

"One coffee, blueberry muffin and yogurt dog treats." Nick set the goods on the table, then slid into the booth opposite Bryn. Her cheeks were still tinged pink, but the tip of her nose was its regular color now. "Warming up?"

"I think you were the one struggling, Dr. Walker." Bryn laughed, then handed a treat to Honey under the table.

"I've run for years but never in such cold conditions. Maybe my next stop should be somewhere warmer."

"Next stop?" Bryn's words were soft, and her green eyes focused on pulling apart the muffin in front of her.

"Yeah." The word was difficult to get out. That was new. He had a mental list of places he wanted to move. It was a running list he'd kept for as long as he could remember. Yet he couldn't pull any of the names to the forefront of his mind. Not while he was sitting here looking at Bryn.

"Ever consider staying?" She cleared her

throat. "Never mind." She waved away the question and shoved a piece of muffin into her mouth.

He didn't want to wave away the question. Didn't want to see the acceptance crossing her face and realize that she expected he'd move.

I will move.

"So, why run outside if you don't like it? There are plenty of gyms around. You don't have to torture yourself in the Boston winter."

"The Santa Dash."

"Ah, Honey and I are running that."

"I assumed that was why you were out this morning." Who would choose to run in such conditions?

"You can go to a gym and run. Honey, however…" Bryn looked under the table, and he could tell she was smiling at the dog before she lifted her head. "The local gyms have some very specific requirements regarding animals on their equipment. Something about the fur."

The atmosphere around them shifted, the uneasy feeling his statement about leaving vanishing. Except there was still an uncomfortable pit in his stomach.

"Golden retrievers are natural runners, and it's a good way to help prevent hip dysplasia. Plus, that way we can crush the Santa Dash." Bryn chuckled as she passed the final dog biscuit to Honey under the table.

"But what will she be wearing for the 5K?"

Nick leaned over, half joking, half serious. Honey was in a warm coat right now, designed for the cloudy cold day, but somehow, he doubted that would be the case for the Santa Dash in a little over a week.

"Her antlers are a big hit with the kids, so that and one of her sweaters." Bryn looked at the dog again, then up at him. "I enjoy dressing her. Maybe it's silly."

"I don't think so."

Bryn beamed at him, her hand starting toward his before pulling back.

Nick's fingers ached to reach over, run his hand over hers, connect whatever was between them. The easiness between them—it was something he'd never experienced.

"We should get going." Bryn tapped her finger, then pulled out her phone.

"Before you go—where's the best place to get a fresh tree?" He didn't decorate for the holidays, but Bryn was rubbing off on him. He'd looked at his place today and decided he needed at least a few things. "And decorations—because I don't technically have ornaments."

"A tree is easy. Mitchell's has fresh ones. Decorations…that's a different story. What kinds of things do you like?" Honey wacked her head against the table, and Bryn looked down.

"She's ready for breakfast and a nap. Why don't we go tomorrow after our shifts at the hospital? It can be a fun night out before I officially start on Friday."

That was the perfect plan. "It's a date."

Date...

The word slipped out, and he knew his eyes were wide.

"I'll see you tomorrow, Nick."

Bryn grabbed Honey's leash and waved a quick goodbye. She hadn't responded to his slip.

That was good. They weren't dating. And tomorrow wasn't a date...so why did it bother him so much that she wasn't even fazed by his response?

CHAPTER SIX

"YOU EXCITED ABOUT TOMORROW?" Izzy, one of the pediatricians on Ward 34, was smiling as she walked out of Beacon.

"Yeah." Bryn nodded. She was excited, and Ailani was right—the nerves were there, but she was ready for this next adventure. "Although it was weird to be here today without Honey."

"I'll admit that it's a little weird not to see you with a ball of golden fluff next to you." Izzy tightened her coat as the chilly air whipped around them. "I bet she'll be happy to see you when you get home."

"That feeling is very mutual." Honey had been her rock after Ethan had walked out. She'd curled herself into Bryn's side, letting Bryn cuddle her as she'd sobbed about the life she'd lost. Coming in for her meetings with HR and orientation without Honey felt a little weird.

"Big plans for tonight? Or are you just relaxing before the big day?"

Big plans... That wasn't a good descriptor for

her night with Nick. How many times had she replayed his words? *It's a date*.

A figure of speech. An easy throwaway statement. They weren't dating. She was helping him put up his Christmas tree—that felt like something.

And maybe if he wasn't already plotting his next place, she might let her heart investigate it further. Some place warm. Nick had been in Boston a little less than a month. Not even long enough to unpack, and yet he was already thinking of the next thing.

Her father was that way. Always thinking of his next score, the next big thing. It never worked out, but that didn't make him change his ways. And Ethan…her ex-husband's focus was always the next step in his career. Neither was ever happy in the here and now. Never happy with her.

"I'm helping Nick—Dr. Walker—find a tree. He wants a real one." Bryn scrunched her nose. She liked the smell of fresh trees, but the fire hazard… Her brain just couldn't ignore it.

"Mitchell's is the place, then. Interesting date idea."

"Mitchell's is what I told him, but it isn't a date." Bryn kept her eyes focused on the parking lot, knowing Izzy's sweet, intuitive gaze was trained on her.

"Picking out a tree is a date—at least according to every holiday movie I have ever seen."

The wind was biting, but Bryn's face was warm. "Well, real life isn't exactly movie magic."

"Isn't that true."

The quiet words made Bryn's head pop up. The faraway look in the pediatrician's eyes sent a rush through Bryn's thoughts. She'd been so lost in her own wanderings about Nick.

"Izzy?"

"This is my car." Izzy's face was bright, though her smile wasn't quite full. "Enjoy your not-date tonight, Bryn. See you tomorrow—on the floor."

Bryn raised a hand and hurried to her own vehicle as the wind cut through the parking structure again. She and Nick would have fun tonight. That didn't make it a date.

Not a date. Not a date. This is not a date.

The fact that Bryn had had to remind herself of that fact as she strolled to Nick's door was not a good sign.

He's leaving. He just got here, and he's already thinking of leaving. Focus on that.

Boston was her place. She'd love to travel, vacation abroad or visit all fifty states, but this city—it was where she felt at peace.

And part of her wished Nick felt that, too.

She raised her hand to knock, not nearly as secure as she wanted to be in her determination that this friendship with Nick was just that. A way to pull her from her hibernation and help him get familiar with Boston before he vanished and started the process all over again.

"Bryn." His smile was infectious, and the invisible chain that seemed to tug on her heart whenever he was around tightened a little further.

"I really can't thank you enough for choosing a tree with me." He closed the door and stepped into the hallway. "No Honey tonight?"

"Oh." Bryn blinked and looked to her side, well aware that she'd left Honey at home but not quite knowing how to respond. "I left her at the apartment. Afraid all you have tonight is just me." Guess that should've cleared up any questions she had about this being a date. No one expected someone to bring their dog, even one they'd trained as a therapy animal, on a date.

"Well, 'just Bryn' is wonderful, too." Nick leaned closer, his spicy scent wrapping through her before he yanked his head back.

For a moment, she'd thought he might kiss her. She'd nearly closed the distance between them. That would've been an embarrassing gaffe.

It didn't happen.

But that she thought it could…

"So, Mitchell's sells the best trees?"

"Yes. And it's close. By the time you find parking, it will probably be easiest to get one we can carry back here on our own."

"That's fine. If you don't mind." Nick buried

his hands into his pockets. No chance of holding hands…which made sense.

So why did it bother her? "Of course not."

"Did you get your tree there?"

"Oh, no. I have a fake fir." The idea of a real tree made her shudder. She'd never have one, not in any place she slept. Not again.

His eyebrows pulled together. "Really? I would've pegged you as a real-tree gal."

"Nope. My mom liked real trees, but the danger with them…" She shrugged as the horrid night their apartment had nearly caught fire ran through her memory.

A week after Christmas, her father had called her mother after Bryn had gone to sleep. Popping in like he did. And like always, her mother had gotten excited that maybe this time was different. Maybe this time he'd stay. He hadn't even wanted to come to the apartment…a red flag her mom should've seen.

But then, who was Bryn to judge missing red flags?

"They aren't dangerous if you keep them watered, make sure the lights aren't on when you aren't around and get rid of them right after Christmas."

"Said like someone who never put a fire out." Bryn laughed, but there was nothing funny about the situation. It was only because she'd gotten up after a bad dream that she'd been awake for the first spark.

"You put a fire out?"

"A small one." She bit her lip. "I was looking for my mom." She hadn't found her, but that wasn't information she needed to share. "There was a little smoke on the tree. I think I thought I was still dreaming. I pulled the lights…which was good because after the spark caught, I threw water on it. The smoke alarm went off, but there wasn't any damage beyond the tree."

"That would make me purchase a fake tree, too." Nick's hand swung by hers.

What would he do if she reached for it?

Bryn mentally shook that thought away. *Not a date…remember.*

She hadn't held hands with anyone in so long. Hadn't really touched someone. It was a funny feeling. She gave hugs and small touches to her patients when they asked. And she'd hugged Nick the other night, held him tightly while he'd dealt with his own internal turmoil. But how long had it been since someone had reached out to her?

Offered her comfort?

The answer was, sadly, far too long.

"Where was your mother?"

His question shook her morose thoughts loose. Unfortunately, there was no happy answer there, either.

"Out with my father. He wasn't…" What were

the best words here? Her father lacked so many things. "Wasn't around much." That was one way to put neglectful, mean, vindictive, absent.

"And not like mine?" Nick's arm slid around her shoulders. "Mine slept at the office far too often, but his home, the one he'd claim—even if he rarely rested there, was ours."

He squeezed her, and she leaned her head against his shoulder. The support he was offering was sweet. "No. Not like yours. Richard Bedford wandered throughout his thirty-six-year marriage. Mom always thought he'd come around. She really loved him. He…he loves himself."

Nick squeezed her one more time, then dropped his arm. Bryn lifted her head, grateful for the comfort, even if she wished he'd hold her a few minutes longer.

"So, you made a good point regarding safety issues. I think maybe we should grab a fake tree. We can pick up some ornaments, too."

"Nick…" Bryn hit her hip against his as she pointed to Mitchell's up the corner. "My issues with real trees don't have to impact what you put in your apartment."

"They don't have to, but…"

The silence that hung on that *but* was nearly deafening.

She wanted to push. Wanted to pull whatever words he wasn't saying into the open.

"But…" He looked at her, his brown eyes staring directly into her soul. "But…"

"Three *buts*. Off to a good start there, Nick."

"Real trees make you nervous, right?"

"Right." Bryn shook her head, not quite understanding where he was going.

"Well, if I plan to have you in my place, you know, for area familiarization and everything, I don't want you to be uncomfortable." Nick's dark cheeks were just a shade darker, and Bryn suspected they were full of heat.

Her cheeks certainly were.

"That's very kind of you."

Nick offered his arm, and she took it as they walked back to his car and headed to grab a tree. A fake tree.

Her throat tightened. It was the kindest thing anyone had done for Bryn in forever.

"It's bright."

Bryn's words were kind, but Nick knew she was searching for more and not finding them. There wasn't a lot you could say. His tree was fine. That was the best descriptor he could use for the blue-and-red monstrosity.

"Why did I only buy red ornaments?"

Her giggle made up for the very un-holiday-looking tree in the corner. "Well, if you had bought a regular green fir-looking one, it would look festive in the traditional way."

"They had blue Christmas trees, Bryn!" He pointed to the tree. How could he possibly choose a plain tree when there were other options? "And purple and orange. I mean, if you're going to have a fake tree, why not go snazzy?"

It would've been a good argument if he'd picked different ornaments.

"Snazzy is great…but the bright red on the electric blue is…a look."

A look was as good descriptor for what was happening in the corner of his apartment. "It *is* a lot."

"Sure." Bryn stepped next to him, tilting her head as she looked at the tree. "I bet it's brighter than any tree you've had before."

"We didn't have trees."

Her head shifted, and her body moved just a bit closer to his. Not quite touching, but close enough to add comfort quickly after his words.

His family celebrated Christmas, just not with much fuss…and that included trees. It was hard to complain when they'd had stockings and piles of presents in the corner.

But presents didn't compensate for growing up alone. Nick wondered if his parents had used so many gifts to make up for not being around, for pushing them to become the picture of service… their vision of service.

"I see."

"Mom was often stationed in different places

than us. Dad…" Nick crossed then uncrossed his arms as he looked at the tree. "Well, Dad's attention wasn't ever very focused on decorations."

Unless we were performing something he could brag about or salute.

Her hand slipped into his, and she squeezed it.

It was nice. No, that wasn't the right descriptor. It was so much more than that. Something had shifted the day he'd met Bryn. It was like his heart had met a kindred soul.

A person it wanted in his life. A person supposed to be in his life. But was that fair when he knew he wasn't planning to stay where Bryn would always feel at home?

And was it selfish that so much of him didn't care? He wanted Bryn in his life. Needed her in a way he couldn't put into words. At least for as long as he stayed in Boston.

"Well, then maybe this is a new tradition for you. Each year, you do your best to add one new Christmas decoration."

"What goes with this tree?" Nick laughed. It really was the opposite of what he'd been going for. But he'd spent the night hanging out with Bryn, so he couldn't get too upset that this tree wasn't like the ones he'd seen in friend's houses and magazines growing up.

The general might not've been big on decorations, but he would hate this one!

Part of Nick wanted to celebrate that. The rebel

in himself. The one who'd bucked the family tradition.

Another part wanted to put the tree back in the box, return it and get something more "traditional." Which wouldn't matter because it wasn't like his father would ever see it.

"There are people that do themes for their decorations. You could make yours the decor version of the ugly Christmas sweater." She giggled, then covered her mouth.

"What's your theme?" Her green eyes caught his, and Nick couldn't look away if he'd wanted to.

The world seemed to hang on this moment. This pinpoint in time that was just for them. The universe holding its breath as they looked at each other.

It was a moment of nothing and everything all at once. Such a fancy phrase. One he'd heard romantics utter some variation of but he'd never experienced it, never believed in its existence.

Until he'd met the woman beside him. How was it possible to share not one but multiple versions of this with a person?

"I don't have one. Not really. Ailani says my decorations make the apartment feel cozy."

Cozy.

What a descriptor. He bet her place felt like a home. Warm and cozy.

"I buy the decorations that make me happy.

My tree is full of these angels. They release a new version each year. My grandmother used to give me one every year as part of my Christmas presents. My ex always got upset because he said the tree was half angels."

Nick put his arm around her waist, and she leaned her head against his shoulder. This should've felt awkward. In theory, they were closer to strangers than anything else. He'd worked with colleagues in med school for four years knowing nothing more than their names and the specialty they'd wanted to practice.

With Bryn, everything felt like a puzzle piece clicking into the perfect place.

"When she passed, my mom continued the tradition, and a few years ago when she died, I bought them for myself."

Because her ex wouldn't.

She didn't say the words, but he could hear them on the edge of the soft tone.

"I haven't bought this year's." She let out a sigh. "With everything from last year and my not-stuck-to plan to ignore the holiday, I never got it. Missing that one won't make much of a difference. Like I said, my tree is nearly full of them."

She needed that ornament. Pure and simple. He wasn't exactly sure where to find it, but he would.

She looked at her watch, and he knew this signal. Bryn was getting ready to leave. It was late, and they'd been together for hours. Yet it wasn't enough time.

He was starting to suspect there might never be *enough* time with Bryn.

"Honey needs to be walked?" His voice was soft, the question hanging between them.

"No. Ailani said she'd handle it." Bryn pursed her lips as her green eyes connected with his.

What would she do if he leaned his head? If he dropped his lips to hers? She was so close. A head tilt, a lowering of the gaze, movement universally acknowledged by lovers as they led up to a first kiss.

"Bryn." Her name on the tip of his tongue made him ache to follow through with the motion.

This was the moment. The one he'd remember forever. Long after he'd left Boston.

The thought was enough to make him start.

And she pulled back. A look passing across her features that he couldn't quite register. Hurt? Or relief?

Nick didn't know. But the moment was lost, and his heart ached that he might never find it again.

"I look forward to seeing you in nursing scrubs, Bryn." He slapped his head with his hand. "I swear that was not the worst pickup line. It was real—"

"A real pickup line?" Her blond brow rose.

"No." Well, he'd found awkward. Found it and dived right past it into the pool of shame.

"I just meant it will be nice to see you on the floor. Nursing. Though I know everyone will miss Honey, too." He blew out a breath, knowing that hadn't salvaged the interaction.

From nearly kissing to sticking both of his feet in his mouth.

"I'll see you tomorrow." She raised her hand, and for the longest second, he thought she might cup his cheek.

If she did, he'd drop his lips to hers and explore whatever was between them.

Instead, she pushed her hand against his shoulder. "It's a nice tree. Bright, but nice. And yours. Good night, Nick."

"Good night, Bryn."

CHAPTER SEVEN

"YOU READY?" Liz's bright smile did little to ease Bryn's mind as she stepped into the locker room. That wasn't the radiologist tech's fault, though.

She was starting nursing today. Stepping back into the role that felt so foreign after Ethan had walked out on their relationship. And once again she was crushing on a coworker.

She'd been so sure Nick was going to kiss her last night. So sure his lips would brush hers. Her body had ached for the moment. Then he'd pulled back.

Hurt and relief had rushed through her all at once. Then she'd had to stop herself from cupping his cheek. Who did that!

Someone who wanted to be kissed.

"Ready as I can be." At least that was true. "My roommate told me adventure can be thrilling and terrifying."

"That's a good line." Liz pulled off her coat.

"I can't believe I'm here without Honey." The hospital was keeping her as a nurse seventy percent and a therapy handler at thirty percent. So she'd still be here one day a week with Honey, but it felt wrong to be here without her furry friend by her side.

"It is a little weird. I know you spend most your time on the pediatric floor, but everyone in the hospital loves her and her cute little outfits."

"How could they not!" Bryn laughed as she searched for her allocated locker. Thinking about Honey almost drove her thoughts away from Nick. Almost.

"Oliver." Liz raised a hand as the other radiology tech pushed through the door. "He's quite the cutie, huh." The last comment was muttered in an undertone.

Liz had waved with such fanfare Bryn couldn't stop the giggle rising in her throat. The radiologist tech was pure fun. It was a shame she didn't get to work with her more. Liz, like Nick, had lived all over. Bryn loved hearing her stories about starting over, finding new things. Ailani had done the same—chosen her own adventure.

Maybe it was something Bryn should investigate more closely. Even if it meant leaving Boston?

Her heart clenched at the idea, and she pushed it aside.

Oliver smiled at Liz, his eyes rooted on her.

It looked like Liz's crush was reciprocated. If only it were as easy for Bryn to read Nick.

Her belly did a little flip as she saw the doctor himself step into the room.

"First day should be pretty easy for you." Liz grinned. "No awkward meeting-your-new-colleagues moments."

"Because everyone already loves Bryn," Nick stated as he eased into the conversation.

"*Love* is a strong word." Bryn knew her cheeks were flaming, and she hoped Nick would chalk it up to nerves from the first day, rather than the mountain of emotions pressing against every nerve in her body as the gorgeous pediatrician stepped to her side.

"But an accurate one," Nick said.

Bryn dipped her head and waited as a Liz and Oliver rushed out with a wave. The air in the small room seemed to evaporate as Nick stood next to her and a small silence descended.

Bryn consciously breathed in and out, hyperaware of the man beside her. Had he thought about last night? Did he even realize she'd thought he was going to kiss her? That she'd wanted it?

Probably not.

Nick had promised to help her step out of her hibernation. He was doing brilliantly, but for reasons she hadn't expected. She was supposed to be stepping back into nursing. Experiencing the holidays…

And instead, it was her heart wakening. That was not supposed to be in the cards.

The windows were open, but the heat between the occupants didn't seem to cool at all.

"I wonder what new treats are in the break room this morning." Nick's eyes were bright as he glanced at her. "It always smells like sugar. Whoever made the molasses cookies was an artist." He put his fingers to his lips, kissing them, then letting his hand open. The gesture was so relaxed. So loose and perfect.

And all Bryn could focus on was his lips. Nick's full, luscious lips that had been so close to hers less than twelve hours ago but not connected.

She needed to focus on something other than the hot doc. Which should've been easy since she was working the floor today. If she was at a new hospital, it might've been, but she knew everyone. This was a new position, not a new job, and those first-day butterflies were not an available distraction from Nick.

"I keep meaning to make iced sugar cookies." The words came out as Bryn slid her bag into her locker. She'd worn her holiday scrubs today. Technically the hospital provided scrubs, but floor nurses could wear their own, if they paid for them.

Like clothes for Honey, Bryn had an entire closet of candy-cane, Santa and cookie scrubs for this time of year. It was festive, and the patients loved it.

"Iced cookies?" Nick leaned his shoulder against the other side of the locker. "Like splattered with icing and sprinkles or fancy decorated?" He raised his brows, his smile ripping through her.

"Fancy." Bryn shrugged. "I told you I used to holiday out! I took a class a few years ago on cookie and cake decorating. They are very pretty. Want to help me make some?"

The question flew out, and she couldn't help the hope that he'd say yes. Maybe that wasn't the smartest move after thinking he'd kiss her, but technically she was showing him around Boston and he was helping her find herself.

"You bet. Though not sure I'll be any help on the frosting side."

"It's how they taste that matters. And people buy the cookies no matter what. After all, Camp Heartlight is a good cause." Bryn shut her locker; it was time to get on with the day.

"It is." He righted himself and smiled. "Have a great first day, Bryn."

"Thanks, Nick."

Bryn was smiling as she stepped into a patient's room. Nick had caught a few glimpses of her today while he'd done rounds. Each time, she'd had a grin on her face.

Nursing was a noble profession. However, Nick thought it was important for people to understand that it was a job. One that should be respected, like all professions. If it was just a job for some individuals, something that they did because it was interesting or made a good wage, that was all right.

For some, though, it was a true calling—the place where their spirit felt most at home.

And Bryn was one of those people. It was why she'd not been able to fully leave the profession after everything that had happened with her ex.

"Dr. Walker?"

Nick turned to greet Dr. Izzy Jeong. "Yes, Dr. Jeong?"

"You treated a patient named Susan Cole—she goes by Susie, right?"

The name sent his spirits tumbling. "Yes. She presented with fainting…" He closed his eyes and tried to think through his days before it clicked. "Exactly a week ago. She was here my first day."

"A week ago. Exactly." Izzy looked at the tablet chart and let out a sigh. "You couldn't identify the cause?"

"No." Nick looked down the hall, not knowing which room was Susie's, but knowing she was here. And that meant she'd fainted again. Another fainting spell meant something was going on. But what?

"Her labs were perfect. Her EKG showed nothing. I told her mother that sometimes fainting spells happen. There is stress in the family."

"What family doesn't have stress?" Izzy tapped a few things out on the tablet.

"True." Everyone had things going on, but there'd been a look on Susie's mother's face. A sadness that had permeated the room. "The father isn't in the picture, but I don't think it's a divorce or dead-beat situation. Susie said she can't video call with him."

"Prison?"

Izzy's suggestion was possible. More than a million children in the US had an incarcerated parent, something that would add stress to any family.

"I don't know. But stress on any body, particularly a little one, could cause a fainting spell. However, more than one a week apart?"

"Not unheard of." Izzy frowned and looked down the hall to the patients' rooms.

"But unlikely." Nick blew out a breath. "I take it she's your patient for this admit?"

Izzy nodded. "I've called for an internal-medicine consult. The blood work the ER did isn't hitting any red flags, and once again, the EKG is perfect."

"I hate this kind of case." Nick crossed his arms, then uncrossed them. People expected doctors to have all the answers. It was why they went to school for so many years. They knew a lot, and usually the answer was discernible.

When it wasn't… A chill sunk through his nerves. They hadn't exhausted the options. He'd not travel the route of worst-case scenarios. Not yet.

Maybe Internal Medicine would crack the case.

"They're sending Kalista Mitchell—second-year resident in Internal Medicine. She should be here within the hour, or so they say."

Nick agreed with the frustration. It wasn't the specialty department's fault. They were in high demand, but when given a time estimate, he often mentally doubled it.

"I hate not being able to give her mom an answer." Izzy's hand ran along her belly, then darted back to the tablet chart.

"Susie's back." Bryn's distressed voice was soft as she stepped next to him.

He must've been worried to miss her walking up. "Dr. Jeong just told me. And once again, she's presenting as fine."

Bryn let out a noncommittal noise. Was she traveling the worst-case-scenario lines, too?

"I've requested a consult from internal-medicine." Izzy looked at Bryn. "She saw Honey—that was in her chart. Did you notice anything when she visited with the dog? I'm grasping at straws, and I understand that."

Bryn closed her eyes and crossed her arms. "She loved Honey. She complained about not being able to video chat with her dad. Her mom seemed stressed. If there was anything else, I don't recall it."

"You and Dr. Walker are on the same wavelength. That's almost word for word what he said." Izzy chuckled.

"Not helpful, but at least our memories are probably accurate." Bryn's eyes caught his, then looked away.

Izzy was right. They seemed to be on the same wavelength, the same chord, the same everything.

"Someone call for an IM consult?" The resident with red hair power walked toward them.

"Yes." Izzy looked a little surprised.

Honestly, Nick was, too. "That was quick. The order went in less than twenty minutes ago."

"I'd just finished with a patient, so could come straight here," Kalista explained. She nodded to Bryn, "It's nice to see you in nurse's scrubs, Bryn, but a little weird not to see a ball of golden fluff at your side."

Bryn gave her a broad smile. "That's what everyone says, Kali. I do sometimes find myself looking at the ground or snapping to bring her to my side. Habit."

"Bryn, can you come with us for the consult?" Izzy looked to Kali. "I really would like to get Susie's mom an answer, if we can."

"Absolutely."

"You'll fill me in?" Nick caught Bryn's gaze before she started off.

"Of course."

"Still no puppy."

Susie crossed her arms and glared at Bryn as she followed Izzy and Kalista through her door. It was the first thing Susie had said when Bryn had come to do vitals check.

"Susan."

The little girl's shoulders slumped as her head hit her chest. Clearly, her full name was only used when Susie was misbehaving.

"Sorry, Susie. Honey stayed home today."

"I want to go home, too."

"Of course you do." Kali slid next to the bed and offered Susie a smile. "My name is Dr. Mitchell. I'm going to ask you and your mom some questions and see if we can figure out why you keep visiting the hospital."

Visiting the hospital.

Bryn loved that terminology. Hospitals were scary places for kids and adults. Visiting seemed to lesson that some. She'd have to steal that line.

"I want to go home, and I want Daddy."

Susie's mother closed her eyes and bit her lip so hard, Bryn feared she was tasting blood. Then she seemed to shake herself and offered her daughter a watery smile. "I know, baby. Me, too."

Bryn looked to Izzy and saw the pediatrician shift her focus to Ellen, too.

"Have you eaten anything this month that's new? Anything you've never eaten before?" Kali asked Susie.

"Sugar cookies. I had sugar cookies. They had sprinkles. One was shaped like a tree, and the other was a round one with red icing. It turned my teeth red."

"You've had sugar cookies before, Susie," her mom interjected. "They just looked like regular cookies instead of Christmas cookies."

"The trees taste better. They do."

"They do." Kali nodded to Susie, then looked to Ellen. "Can you think of any new food introductions?"

"No. I haven't had a lot of time to experiment. It's been mostly boxed mac and cheese and hot dogs."

"Mac and cheese is one of my favorites, too." Kali's words were bright and directed to Ellen.

Bryn knew parents feared judgment when their kids were in the hospital. That parent blogs and social media had made some feel inadequate if they couldn't make a homemade three-course feast three times a day with organic fruits and veggies.

Kids needed love and attention. Mac and cheese was fine.

"All right, so no new food introductions. Tell

me what was happening right before each fainting incident."

"I wanted raisins and to talk to Daddy."

Kali tilted her head as she looked at Susie. Kali had posed the question to Ellen, but Susie answering was fine, too. It also meant that she remembered the incidents.

"How did you feel then?" Izzy directed her question at Susie but looked toward Ellen briefly.

"Mad. I know that's bad, but I feel mad sometimes."

"Being mad isn't bad," Ellen's voice was tired, and Bryn stepped beside her. Susie's mother looked like she needed to sleep for three days and then spend a week at a day spa.

Unfortunately, there was no way for Bryn to offer such relief. If Honey were here, she could park her right next to Ellen and let her pet the dog. It wouldn't clear all the stress, but it would help.

"That's right." Kali added, "It's an emotion we all get. But when you were mad, did your body feel anything?"

Susie's eyebrows narrowed. "It felt like my body." The tone was one only a small child could offer. Like she thought the adults were asking the dumbest things.

"I know it sounds like a silly question." Kali winked, then looked at Izzy. "The EKG was fine?"

"Yes. And we ran another this morning."

Kali nodded, then pulled a sticker out of her pocket. "Thank you for answering my questions, Susie."

"No other doctor gave me a sticker." She ripped the back off and stuck it to her gown, her grin brilliant.

If she hadn't fainted twice, Bryn would say Susie was in perfect health.

Kali looked to Izzy, then to Ellen. "I'm going to run my thoughts by my attending. They will be in sometime later to talk to you."

"Thank you." Ellen nodded, but Bryn could see the frustration pooling in her. She wanted answers, and the two doctors didn't have one.

"Will they have stickers?"

"I don't know, Susie, but I'll let them know you like stickers." Kali offered the little one a smile.

"And dogs. I like dogs."

Bryn had to cover her lips to keep from laughing. There was no way to promise Susie that she'd bring Honey to see her. With luck, Susie wouldn't be here the next time she had the therapy dog.

"I'll tell Honey you said hi when I get home." Bryn could tell Susie didn't like that answer, but she didn't argue as the medical professionals left for the hallway.

"So, what are you planning to tell your attending?" Izzy's voice was tight. "Because I want to give Ellen some idea of what is happening if we can."

"Honestly, I wonder if it's heart related. She looks very healthy. Many things can cause fainting. Lung and brain cancer, kidney disease to list just a few of the most dangerous, but it can also be brought on by stress and is fairly easy to correct."

"The mad comment?" Bryn raised a brow. It didn't surprise her that Susie didn't have words to describe how her body felt. At five, it would have to be a big pain moment. That it wasn't… well, that was actually a good thing. Though it added to the mystery of the diagnosis.

"An EKG only catches the heart in real time. Not a previous episode. I'm Internal Medicine. I'm not saying it isn't an infection or a chronic condition, but I think ruling out heart conditions is step one."

"Any idea how long the wait is to get a pediatric cardiologist? With multiple clear EKGs, she doesn't qualify to see one here. And pushing it as a priority will be a difficult sell with the insurance company." Izzy looked like she wanted to stamp her feet.

Bryn knew she was frowning. The fact that insurance and a patient's ability to pay were such drivers was difficult for most medical professionals, but it was an unfortunate part of the medical systems.

"Maybe my attending will have a better answer. I'll talk to them, hopefully get some answers soon." Kali walked off, and Izzy leaned against the wall.

"You all right?"

Izzy was usually bright and sunshiny, but she looked a little worn today. Maybe it was just Susie, but Bryn wondered if there was something else.

"Just a little tired."

"'Tis the season." Holiday cheer wasn't the only thing passed around this time of year, after all.

"True." Izzy smiled, but Bryn could see that it was an effort.

"You'll let me know if you need anything?"

"Of course. Thanks for checking, Bryn." She pushed off the wall and headed to her next patient.

Bryn looked at the closed door, wishing there was something she could do for Ellen and Susie, but coming up with a big fat nothing.

CHAPTER EIGHT

"FIRST DAY OVER!" Nick beamed as Bryn stepped beside him to wait for the elevator.

"It is." Bryn closed her eyes for a moment. "It was a good day, other than not finding an answer on Susie's fainting spells."

"Izzy told me they're recommending Susie see a cardiologist."

Bryn blew out a breath as she looked back over her shoulder.

The first day was always exhausting. He was glad that Izzy had filled in the information for him. But he also understood how unsettling a shift without answers for a patient was.

Kali's attending agreed that a heart condition needed to be ruled out before they went further down the medical-oddity list of conditions. They also thought it was safe to discharge her with orders to follow up with a pediatric cardiologist.

Nick didn't know if Ellen had been told that yet, but assuming her vitals remained stable, Susie was going home soon—again.

Hopefully, she wouldn't be back at Beacon. It was one of the weird things about this job. You got close to patients, helped them on the road to health and then, if you were lucky, you didn't see them again.

The elevator doors opened, and Nick frowned. He hadn't gotten to see Bryn much on the floor—the nature of the job keeping them busy. And he wasn't quite ready to say good-night.

They started toward the parking garage, and he wondered if it was too much to ask if she wanted to grab a drink or some dessert after a long day.

"Just answer your damn phone!"

Bryn was moving before he could quite register who'd called out.

"Ellen." Bryn's tone was commanding but gentle. "Ellen."

Susie's mother turned, and Nick's heart broke at her red eyes and tear-stained cheeks.

Bryn didn't say anything else. She just opened her arms. Ellen waited only a microsecond before stepping into them and bursting out sobbing. Bryn held her.

And Nick waited. He wasn't sure his presence would be helpful, but until he knew why she was so upset, he wasn't leaving.

"So-sorry." A sob broke the word as Ellen stepped back and wiped at her eyes. The action wouldn't do much, but it was a comforting motion.

"It's fine." Bryn's voice was soft now, the understanding nurse rather than the commanding one. "Nick—Dr. Walker—and I didn't have any plans. Right?"

"Nope. No plans." He'd been trying to think of one, but that wasn't the point right now.

"Were you trying to get a hold of your husband?"

"Oh." Ellen crossed her arms around her waist. She looked tiny and so worn out. "No. Jack can't…" Her words trailed off. "He's not available right now."

Not available right now.

Such a cool statement. One that could have dozens of meanings.

"I was actually trying to reach one of our senators." Ellen let out a bitter laugh. "Not that they ever answer. That voicemail won't see one of their staffers reaching out. Though all of my polite requests haven't gotten me return phone calls, either."

"Is there anything we can do?" Bryn looked at Nick, and he shrugged.

If Ellen was calling senators, he didn't know what the two of them might be able to do. His father was connected to more politicians than anyone else Nick knew. But that level of contact was reserved for so few. It was the reason his father's military consulting business made so much money following his retirement.

"Either of you know the president?" Ellen pulled on her neck, then looked at her watch.

"No," Bryn and Nick said at the same time.

"Why do you need the president?" Nick wasn't sure why Susie's mother would need to contact senators, let alone ask if they knew the president in a way that he was fairly sure was a joke but also a hopeful statement that maybe, just maybe, she might get lucky.

"It doesn't matter." Ellen shook her head. "I need to get back before Susie wakes up. If I'm not there, she'll worry."

She looked at Bryn. "Thank you for the hug—I didn't realize how much I needed it." Then she headed back inside before either he or Bryn could say anything else.

"What just happened?"

"Honestly... I have no idea." Nick looked at the closed hospital doors, not sure what to make of this encounter. "But your reaction was perfect. She needed that hug."

"Just doing my job."

But she wasn't on the clock. It was like Bryn instinctively knew what people needed and acted to ensure they got it. It was admirable, but he suspected it was also exhausting.

"Any chance you want to grab a drink?"

Her question sent most of the worries about Ellen from his mind. "I'd love one."

"Great." She made a face, and he held his breath. "Oh no. I need to go home—Honey."

"I understand." And he did. Honey had been home by herself today. He was sure Bryn had worked out a way for the dog to get fed and walked, but that wasn't the same as having her person home.

"Do you want to get a drink at my place? I have wine."

Nick couldn't think of anywhere else he'd rather be. "Point me in the direction and I'm there."

Bryn pulled out her phone, and a few seconds later his phone dinged. "That's the address. Give me an hour, then…" She shrugged, and there was a hint of color in her cheeks.

"I'll see you soon." Nick thought he might be dancing on air as he headed for his car.

Bryn's hair was still wet as she looked in the mirror and assessed the fourth outfit she'd thrown on after taking Honey out for a walk and grabbing the quickest shower known to humankind. Maybe she should have told Nick to give her two hours.

That would only have given her more time to overthink the outfit she was wearing.

Ailani was out tonight, but still. Her place! What had she been thinking?

It had just seemed like such a natural response. One her heart had offered before her brain could work through any of the potential complications.

So now she was standing in front of her mirror in a plain white T-shirt and comfy athleisure pants, wondering if she was too dressed down for this. Maybe a pair of jeans…but she was off work and just wanted to relax, and that meant no buttons.

Still… Bryn started toward the closet when her phone buzzed.

Here.

Such a simple text, but her heart skipped a beat. She looked at the pants and huffed. Honey tilted her head at the noise, and Bryn petted the dog's head before heading to the door. "I guess this will have to work."

She opened the door and nearly let out a sigh as Nick stood before her in a light blue T-shirt and jeans that hugged his waist so perfectly.

"Hi, Honey." Nick bent down and rubbed the dog's ears.

Bryn's face heated—she'd been worried about what she was wearing, and the first thing Nick had noticed was the dog.

It's a good thing, Bryn.

This was a simple crush. One she needed to push past. Nick was a coworker and one that rambled to new places when the urge to run struck. A man she could fall for. So easily. And that just meant getting her heart broken.

One heartbreak per life was more than enough.

"Why don't you come in? If you sit on the couch, you can give Honey all the love while I get the wine."

Nick stepped into the apartment and immediately moved toward the tree. "So, these are the angels?"

"Oh." Bryn moved to stand beside him as he gazed at her tree. It was a hodgepodge of ornaments. No theme—angels from her grandmother and mother, a few penguins she'd found funny and ornaments some children at Brigham had made her.

"It's homey and much cuter than mine."

"Well—" Bryn chuckled "—it's certainly not as loud."

Nick's hip bumped hers, and desire pushed through her. How did he kiss? With softness… or a possessive drive that made you forget all your thoughts and sink into a need that was simply Nick?

Her body burned, with no outlet for release. "Do you prefer red or white?"

"Whichever you like."

Bryn shook her head. "You really should choose. I prefer sweet reds. The brand I like is pretty cheap. And it's not for everyone. I remember the first time I poured it for…" Her words cut off.

Ethan wasn't here, and it didn't matter that he'd

flipped out that she'd buy such cheap wine, never mind that she enjoyed it.

"I always keep a few bottles for guests that are nicer quality."

Nick was frowning, the deep lines in his forehead making her nervous. She'd gotten good at reading Ethan's and her mother's moods. Bryn knew exactly what each frown meant, what the smile that was just a tad off indicated.

"Are you all right? If I did…"

"Bryn, I'm not your ex. Who, honestly, if I met the man, I'd say some pretty sharp things to."

"Oh. I know you aren't." That wasn't something Bryn worried over. Nick was about as far away from Ethan as possible. She just wanted him to feel welcome in her home. Wanted…

The urge to clear her throat pulled at her, but Bryn just smiled.

"You watch my moods, don't you?" Another expression she couldn't read passed across his gorgeous features.

"I watch everyone's moods. Nurse superpower." This wasn't a big deal.

Nick raised a brow but didn't comment. "The sweet red is fine. I'm here for the company."

Honey pressed her head against his thigh and let out a soft bark.

"Honey." Bryn pursed her lips as the dog laid a good portion of her weight against Nick. "That isn't polite. Though he came for your company."

"I came for yours. Honey is just an added fluffy perk."

She moved into the kitchen, grabbed the glasses and poured. When she came back into the living room, Nick was looking at one of the angel ornaments.

"You're really fascinated with the angels." She handed him the glass, very conscious of his fingers touching hers.

The heat of the connection, the look in his dark eyes. If energy fields were real, she was certain that hers and Nick's would burn brightly every time they were near each other.

"They're important to you."

She bit her bottom lip as she felt it tremble. Four words. Four words no one ever said to her. Her mother had loved her. Bryn had never doubted her, but she'd been an extension of her father in some ways—something that had kept her mom tethered, for better or worse, to a man she'd loved but who couldn't love her back.

"You can see that whoever is designing them has changed their art over time. The more recent ones," Nick held up the box with last year's date, "have much more descriptive faces versus this one." He pointed to the oldest in her collection.

"Yeah." Bryn took a sip of her wine, the sweet taste hitting her tongue. "I don't have the oldest one. It came out the year I was born, and my grandmother didn't start my collection until my first birthday. I looked for it once. You can find them, but the few that are out there are true collector's items."

Nick made a face, then, in a joking voice, said, "Unopened, new in box."

Bryn giggled. "Yes. Exactly."

"I had a friend in college that loved this comic character—not sure which one. But he'd go to conventions and always get frustrated. The prices put a lot of the collectors' items out of reach for those that truly loved the comic."

"It can seem like a status symbol. Though who would think Christmas ornaments would be so desirable?"

"True." Nick winked. "So now we have something very serious to discuss."

Her breath caught in the back of her throat. "We do?" Was he going to broach the heat between them?

"What day are we frosting cookies, and do you want to do it at my place or yours?"

Bryn knew her mouth was hanging open. Every thought had left her brain. Her mind knew she needed to say something. Anything.

Cookies. She was thinking of kisses. Of running her hands over his glorious body. Trailing her mouth across his jaw. And he was thinking of cookies for the bake sale.

What was she supposed to say? Something.

She needed to say something. Like now. Words. She needed words.

Speak!

Wow, the silence was really deafening.

"We *are* baking cookies, right?"

"Yeah. Of course. Umm… Frosted cookies need to be baked the day before. I can bake them tomorrow. Then we can decorate them the day after. You have the bigger kitchen, so I can just bring them there. And Honey won't get in our way."

There—she'd said the words. Forced them out. Now it was time to change the subject.

"So, why don't we watch a movie? I've been dying to watch a sappy made-for-television movie."

"Operation Get Bryn to Celebrate Christmas is working." Nick beamed as he moved with her. "I love watching movies after a long day. It's my top way of relaxing."

She nodded, not quite trusting herself to speak the truth. Holiday movies were the last thing on her mind—it was just the first thing she'd thought of. But putting on a movie would keep the conversation down, lessen the chance she might say something embarrassing or, worst of all, confess her crush.

She grabbed the remote and saw a look pass over his face as she slid into the oversized chair next to the couch. Was he disappointed she was in the chair? Or was Bryn was reading into something, hoping…?

CHAPTER NINE

COOKIES. NICK HAD asked Bryn about when they would be decorating cookies. Two days later and he still wanted to slap himself. That was the exact opposite of the question he'd wanted to ask.

He'd wanted to ask if he could kiss her. If she felt the heat between them. If she thought of him as often as he thought of her. If her life felt right when he was with her.

If the answer was no, he'd move past it. She was a person he wanted in his life.

The other night had been the perfect opportunity, and he'd misstepped from moment one. Bending down to look at Honey, to keep from telling her how beautiful she'd looked. How tempting the relaxed outfit had been.

Then he'd asked about cookies, and she'd sat in the chair instead of beside him during the movie. The one good thing was he now knew exactly which kind of angel ornament he was looking for.

At least she was coming to his place after

this shift. Cookie decorating and maybe another chance…

"Dr. Walker?"

Nick turned to greet Dr. Iain MacKenzie, the man's thick Scottish accent always reminding him of the year his father had been stationed in England. He still wasn't sure what his father's job in North Yorkshire had been, but Nick had gotten to cross the border into Scotland nearly every weekend. The country was beautiful, and the people were exceptionally welcoming. It was one of his favorite places.

"You're taking over for me on this shift."

"Yep. You ready to head home?"

"So ready." Iain's voice was strained, so that meant there'd been a difficulty. Twelve-hour shifts were long no matter how they went, but some were longer than others.

"The patient in room three—Logan Anderson, sixteen. There's a surgeon coming from Brigham. His mother requested a second opinion regarding the surgery Dr. Lowes recommended for his broken tibia."

"A second opinion on a broken bone?" Second opinions weren't unheard of, and Nick encouraged them for difficult diagnoses. However, a broken bone rarely required one.

Iain nodded. "Dr. Lowes isn't thrilled. I guess it's a pretty cut-and-dry break. They need to put pins in to stabilize."

"And the sooner, the better." Bones tried to stitch themselves back together when they broke, and the process moved even faster in small limbs since kids hadn't stopped growing. If the bones started healing, the surgeon would have to re-break the bone to get it set—extending the healing time.

"That's what Dr. Lowes said. However, the mother is insisting and called the surgeon. A Dr. Pierson—know him?"

"No." Boston had twenty-five hospitals and twenty medical centers. There were doctors, surgeons, nurses and just about every other medical profession all over the city. Even if he'd been in the city for years, it was unlikely he'd know a quarter of the medical professionals outside of his own colleagues.

"Dr. Pierson is the best—at least according to Logan's mother. She wants him to look at the break and see if he'll accept the transfer to Brigham."

"Can't she just request a transfer? Patient's rights?" Nick looked at the notes on the tablet chart. Logan had broken his left leg in a skateboarding incident. He and another skateboarder had collided at an indoor track, and the other kid had landed on his leg at just the right angle.

"The parents are going through a divorce. His dad brought him here because it's the closest."

"Ah." Nick finished reading over the notes. Divorce was hard, even when people felt they were better off separated. When it wasn't amicable and children were involved, he'd seen some terrible things done for "the child's best."

"Does his mom feel Brigham is the better hospital, or is she mad at Dad?"

"Not sure, but she has primary custody. There's another twist—Dr. Pierson doesn't take every case. He's very much sought-after."

"I see." Nick barely controlled his desire to roll his eyes. Most physicians went into medicine to help patients. To solve complicated cases and bring people hope.

A not-insignificant number went in for prestige. Those were sometimes selective in the patients they took on—a way to add to that "prestige." It was something Nick had witnessed a handful of times but never understood.

"Not sure when he'll be here. I've instructed the nurses to keep Logan as comfortable as possible." Iain looked toward the room and frowned.

"We got it from here. Hopefully by the next time you're on shift, all this will be worked out without Logan going through the pain of transferring and he'll have had surgery and be getting ready for physical therapy." It would be nice to think that Logan might be discharged by then, but unfortunately an orthopedic break requiring pins likely meant the teen would be at the hospital for a while.

Iain nodded, looked at the room's closed door once more, then back at Nick. "Good luck."

"Thanks."

Bryn slipped out of room three, and Nick's feet moved before he could think through what he was going to say.

"How is Logan?"

Her green eyes seemed to look through him as she shrugged her shoulders.

"Bryn?"

"He's sleeping. Not overly restful, given his raised leg and the pain that even powerful narcotics won't fully dim."

"That's the best we can hope for, at least according to what Iain told me. So what's wrong?" Because something had upset her.

"His mother is difficult."

"Iain mentioned that as well." Bryn started down the hall, but Nick reached out and grabbed her arm. His touch was light and brief, but he wanted to pull her into his arms. Whatever the mother had said, it must have been short. "Bryn. Talk to me."

She looked at the place where his hand had just been, then ran a hand over where he'd touched. "Mom wants her son at Brigham. She thinks we're all mediocre, for reasons that don't bear repeating, and she's upset that her son is so heavily medicated."

"He has a compound fracture." Nick blinked, knowing his face must've been a mixture of horror and shock. What parent wouldn't want their child as comfortable as possible in this situation?

"He does. But she's focusing on making a point to her soon-to-be ex-husband."

"A point. What point could that possibly be?" Fury rattled through him as he took a deep breath. His parents' union had been unique. Most marriages would not have survived the distance and sometimes years apart. It certainly wasn't the type of union Nick would want, but it seemed to work for them. And his parents would never have proved a point to each other by weaponizing their children.

"That he needs her. That without her people get hurt, that he isn't capable." Bryn looked over his shoulder back at the room. "It's clear she's using Logan as a pawn. It's the image of the family, though, I think. Not love that she's upset about. But then, I don't know, she just screamed at me, not at her husband—who wasn't in the room, and asked why her son was so sleepy."

That was a piece of intel that was good to know. "At least most parents aren't concerned with the family image."

She let out a sound that caused Nick's head to swivel. "Far too many see their children as pawns for the union they want. Not for the individuals they are."

"Bryn…" His heart broke at her tone. It felt like this wasn't about a difficult mother. At least not Logan's difficult mother. "Bryn," he repeated when she didn't look up, "you're enough." He wasn't sure what else to say.

Her eyes lifted, and she offered him a smile, though it was far from the brilliant one he saw so often in his dreams these days. "Thanks." She let out a sigh and looked back at the door. "I'm going to grab a quick cup of coffee in the cafeteria and push off this mood. I'll be back in ten minutes, all right?"

"We still on for cookies?" He understood that she needed a breather. Hell, there were days when all you could muster was a few minutes in the corner of the break room, but you took it—gathered the feelings patients brought up and moved forward.

"We'd better be. I have two dozen stars and two dozen trees we're supposed to make pretty." She nodded, then started down the hall. She looked back over her shoulder once, and he offered her a wave.

"You the one in charge of Logan Anderson?"

The gruff tone had to have come from Dr. Pierson. If the doctor took Logan and his mother signed the paperwork to move him, it would make the lives of everyone who was dealing with

Logan's case easier. But based on Bryn's statement, Nick wasn't sure that was the best choice for the teen.

"Dr. Walker." He held out his hand as he turned. The tall white doctor didn't bother to offer his.

"Dr. Pierson, surgeon at Brigham Women's Hospital." His eyes held no friendly camaraderie, no warmth. "The patient?"

Perhaps he was an accomplished surgeon, but his mannerisms didn't make the best first impression. "He's in room three. Dr. MacKenzie got the full report from our ortho—"

"His mother called me. He has a fractured tibia. Not my usual case."

Usual case.

Nick hoped his face didn't display the disgust that statement brought. Private practice afforded doctors more choice in the types of patients they saw, but most used it to control how much time they had and to lower their caseload. Not to see a certain "type" of case.

"Do you specialize in ankles?" That might explain the frustration he saw from Dr. Pierson. If he specialized in ankles, he could do the tibia reconstruction, but it wouldn't be his typical case. Nick was trying to find something to let him give the surgeon at least some grace.

Anything.

"I specialize in complicated cases." Dr. Pierson cleared his throat. "Where is the patient?"

"Room three. His mother and father are with him."

Dr. Pierson walked off, and Nick moved with him. According to Iain, he had privileges at Beacon, but there was something about the doctor that made Nick uncomfortable. An air that screamed, *Not a good bedside manner.* Logan and his father had been through enough with the bad break—another ear to hear what the surgeon had to say wouldn't be a terrible thing.

"Nina." Dr. Pierson nodded to Logan's mother as he came into the room. The surgeon stepped to the side of the bed but didn't acknowledge Logan.

"Ethan, I'm so happy you made it."

Ethan? The name buzzed in the back of Nick's brain, but he couldn't quite understand why. He looked at the clock. A full minute in the room and Dr. Pierson had still not introduced himself to Logan.

"Yes, well…" Dr. Pierson let out a sigh. "Craig made sure I knew you wanted me to take a look. You could have asked for him, after all he is also an orthopedic surgeon—though not as good as me. Anyway, since he is looking for a new partner for his practice, I decided to indulge him."

"Yes. He and I have grown close." Nina's eyes shifted to her soon-to-be ex-husband.

Nick knew his eyes were wide, and Logan's father made eye contact with him. The man looked as horrified as Nick felt.

Logan needed surgery to set his leg, to make sure it healed properly. That was what mattered here, not some quid pro quo.

"Our divorce will be finalized in a few weeks." Logan's father sighed. "What matters is Logan's leg and getting him cared for."

"Which is what we're doing, Jeff." Nina offered a smile she didn't even attempt to make real. "You have your girl, and I am—"

"Linda is a colleague, not my girl—" Jeff held up his hands. "Nope. We aren't having this conversation. Dr. Pierson, thank you for coming. Are you going to take Logan's case?"

"No."

"Ethan!"

"Nina, this is a simple reconstruction—there is no need for my services. Transporting him will be painful and potentially do more damage."

Finally, something that was about the patient. Nick made a note in the tablet chart. Hopefully Logan could have surgery tomorrow at the latest.

"Simple!" Her face turned bright red, and she shook her fist in the air. "I will tell Craig."

"I'm sure you will, and I will ensure he understands that he's being used to make your husband jealous. Everyone will understand what is happening." Dr. Pierson's words were cool, but the daggers were clear in the tone.

"Have a good afternoon." He dipped his head, then turned and left without another word.

"When will my son get the surgery?" Jeff looked drained as he typed something out on his phone.

"Are you letting your lawyer know, still hoping for more custody?" Nina typed something out on her cell phone, not even looking at her son.

"I'm letting the office know that I won't be in for a few more days. And yes, I will use this with the lawyers. I'm thankful Logan slept through this, but he should be our priority."

"I'll make sure someone updates you when possible." Nick wanted out of the room, it was uncomfortable. He felt for Logan, but at least his father seemed focused on the boy.

He closed the door and saw Dr. Pierson at the end of the hall, leaning against the wall, his back to Nick. The posture made it clear he was talking to someone.

The surgeon had privileges at the hospital, but there was something about his posture, as if his purpose was intimidation.

Suddenly Bryn tried to step around him, but Ethan moved, blocking her.

Ethan.

The name clicked as Bryn's eyes met Nick's from across the distance. Ethan Pierson. Her exhusband. The man who'd dumped her on their honeymoon.

Nick's feet were moving before he could think through his plan. Get to Bryn. Nothing else mattered.

"I see you've gone back to wearing ridiculous scrubs."

It was only as Bryn heard the words coming out of her ex-husband's mouth that her brain finally registered that he was here. At her hospital, looking at her with the same disappointed eyes.

A look that once would have sent her mind into overdrive trying to figure out what slight she must have done. She'd bent herself backward trying to be the perfect version of the wife Ethan had wanted. Broken herself to be what he'd desired. Bryn hadn't liked herself then, though she hadn't wanted to admit it. And it hadn't made Ethan love her, either.

So it didn't matter that he didn't like her fun scrubs. Not anymore.

Still, she felt her shoulders turn in, and the urge to make herself smaller hovered in her chest. The desire to apologize pulled at the back of her throat. Bryn wouldn't give into that, though. Not this time.

She liked the scrubs and so did the children. That was enough. But she also wasn't going to debate it with her ex-husband.

"If you'll excuse me, Ethan." She started to

go around him, but he shifted, catching her just off guard.

Why was there no one in the halls? She swore this place was always busy, but it felt deserted now, when she needed someone…anyone!

"It's good to see you, Bryn." The tone was disingenuous, but if anyone passing heard it, they likely wouldn't think anything of it.

"Do you need something?" She was proud that she hadn't said *It's good to see you, too*. If the raise of his brow was an indicator, he'd expected that. Good. He deserved to be the one feeling out of control for once.

"I was seeing a patient. Broken leg that needs surgery. Basic stuff, really. At least for me."

Making a boy's trauma about himself. How typical. He hadn't even said the patient's name. Honestly, he might not've known it.

Logan. The teen who'd barely woken when she'd entered his room, despite his mother's constant complaints. And he'd tried to make his mother feel better, even exhausted and in pain.

How many times had she done that with her mother—tried to ease a pain that she couldn't ease? A pain her mother had held on to because letting it go would be even more painful.

"Logan." Bryn cleared her throat. "His name is Logan."

"I didn't check." That confirmation did not make her feel better. The same old Ethan.

"It's the bones that matter."

Bryn didn't bother to respond to that.

"Excuse me." She moved to the side, and her eyes caught Nick just before her ex's body cut him off from view.

Had Ethan always been this controlling? Maybe. Or maybe she'd just done whatever he'd asked.

That still makes him controlling, Bryn.

Ethan was too tall for her to see over his shoulder, but she hoped Nick was on his way. Things had been awkward since she'd thought he might kiss her, but she wanted him right now.

And only him.

"It's interesting seeing you in scrubs again. I thought you hung up your stethoscope after our divorce."

The harsh look in his eyes sent a chill down her spine. Their union had set a land-speed record from the altar to divorce court, but she still wished him well. Hoped that whatever it was he was looking for, he found.

She'd assumed he'd think the same for her. Apparently the age-old statement regarding assuming was far too accurate.

"It's new. I'm getting myself back—stethoscope included." It felt good to say.

So good.

"Bryn!" Nick's voice was bright as he pulled her to him, his lips pressing against hers possessively for just a moment before pulling back. "You were right—the blood work came back on Paisley. Thank you!"

She didn't know what to say. There was no patient named Paisley. No blood work. Nick was stepping in with flair.

"Sorry." Nick winked at Bryn before looking at Ethan.

Her ex-husband's cheeks were bright red. The relaxed posture he'd used to trap her had vanished into a rigid man oozing jealousy. He didn't want her…but he didn't want her to want someone else.

Well, too damn bad!

"We've been working on that case for a week, and Bryn…she's amazing."

Ethan opened his mouth, but Nick didn't wait for him to say anything.

"We still on for tonight, angel?"

"You know we are." Bryn smiled back, grateful for the gift he'd given her. Witnessing a speechless Ethan was priceless.

"When you get a moment, can you meet me in room seven? I need to discuss the results with Paisley's father."

And now he'd made a point of getting her away from Ethan. Nick was exactly what she needed… in more ways than one.

"Of course." Bryn nodded, knowing the room was empty.

Nick strolled off, and she didn't bother to hide her grin. Let Ethan think what he wanted.

"You're seeing someone?"

Bryn looked at him, finally seeing the monster she'd cried so many tears over. He wasn't owed any of her life. He'd given that up when he tossed his ring onto the bedside table on their honeymoon.

"That's not any of your business, Ethan." It was shocking how easy the words were, even though her brain was screaming, *Screw you.* "I've moved on. I suggest you do the same."

His mouth opened, but like Nick, she didn't stay to hear what he had to say. All her ex-husband's words had been exhausted—at least as far as she was concerned.

Her fingers ran along her lips. A kiss at the hospital wasn't exactly professional. And if anyone had seen it, she might've been a little perturbed. Though, honestly, probably not.

She'd thought of kissing Nick for the last week—really, since the moment she'd laid eyes on him.

Her only gripe about the encounter was how short the connection had been. But it had been powerful.

Possessive—but in the best way, like he'd claimed her, showed Ethan he had no power.

And he didn't. Not anymore. Nick had tossed the last of her reserve away when she'd met him.

It was like he'd pulled the final cord on the box and let the real Bryn out.

That transformation was the reason there was a stethoscope in her pocket. The reason she'd pulled out her fun scrubs and decorated her tree the way she wanted to for the first time in years.

She was stepping into herself for the first time since she'd moved out of her mother's place, and she liked herself.

"Is he gone?" Nick's question was out before Bryn fully opened the door to room seven.

"He is. Listen, Nick—"

"I'm so sorry, Bryn. I shouldn't have kissed you. That was inappropriate. If you want to report me to Human Resources, I understand."

Nick's words sucked the heat from her body.

"It's fine." She heard the words leave her mouth, but her body locked down. Bryn was tumbling. The place she'd thought they'd been, the reason…

An apology. The first thing he'd given was an apology. And an offer to report himself to Human Resources.

Not a comment on how it had been too short. Or how it was a shame they'd had to have her ex-husband force the issue, even though it felt like they'd been moving to this point from moment one.

He leaves.

She was just supposed to help him adjust to

Boston. It wasn't Nick's fault she was crushing on him. He'd broken up the encounter with Ethan in such a way that she'd never have to worry about him again. That should've been enough.

"Bryn."

She plastered on a smile. "It's fine, Nick. Better than fine. Ethan looked gobsmacked. I've never seen him speechless. Best early Christmas gift ever."

"And the kiss?"

What was she supposed to say? He'd apologized for it. So quickly.

"Was a kiss." That was an answer…not a great one, but better than blurting out that she'd wished it had been longer. That it had happened outside the hospital. In a place where they could explore.

"I'll see you tonight, all right?" She smiled but didn't wait for his response as she pulled on the door to leave.

Today had already been too much, and somehow she had to put her mask back on before they decorated cookies tonight. Maybe the kiss had been inappropriate. A thing to apologize for.

But Bryn had enjoyed it. And she craved more. So much more.

CHAPTER TEN

"THAT IS A lot of cookies." Ailani laughed as she helped Bryn pack up the last of the supplies for tonight's decorating extravaganza.

"It is." Bryn looked at the cookies, the icing, the little baggies she was planning to drop two cookies into apiece. "But it's for a good cause."

"Did you get any of Kali's solstice cookies?" Ailani closed her eyes and sighed. "They were so good. I could have eaten a dozen of them, but they were gone when I went back."

"I missed them. I had some of Leigh's lemon cookies, though. Very good."

"Well, I'm sure these will be delicious." Ailani followed Bryn down to the garage. "Think Nick has a knack for cookie decorating?"

"I don't know, but he seems to really want to try."

"Or…he wants to spend time with you."

The cool garage couldn't stop the heat flooding her cheeks. "He *does* want to spend time with me. As a friend."

"Uh-huh." Ailani chuckled. "The way he looks at you, like he's contemplating kisses… I'm sure friendship is exactly what's on his mind."

"Javi looks at you, too. I've seen it…when you walk by and aren't looking. More than friendly, some might say."

Now it was color flooding Ailani's cheeks. "I hope you have fun decorating, Bryn."

So they were officially disregarding this conversation. That was all right with her. After all, Nick had kissed her this afternoon, then promptly apologized.

"I don't know when I'll be back. Cookie decorating…"

"I've got Honey. Enjoy yourself. No one has a curfew tonight." Ailani waved before darting back to the stairwell.

Maybe she didn't want to hear Bryn's retort, or perhaps she was worried Bryn might bring up Javi again.

The man looked at Ailani. It was sweet, like he was thrilled she'd landed at his hospital. Which, if one thought of it, the odds of finding someone you connected with were so small. It was why her mother had tried so hard, too hard, to keep her father.

And it was the reason Bryn had tried to mold herself to fit Ethan's perfectionist ideal. Billions of people in the world and only one or two were really meant for you.

A fraction so small it was amazing anyone ever found lasting love. Nick's teddy-bear-brown eyes popped into her brain.

She cleared her throat and started the ignition. Her car rumbled to life, and she turned on the radio station that played holiday music twenty-four hours a day for the entire month of December.

Bryn belted out the tunes she loved, hoping they might ease the tension in her belly and knowing there was nothing that was going to stop her brain from thinking about Nick.

"I admit I didn't think there'd be so many cookie supplies." Nick's chuckle rumbled through her as he grabbed the bags of decorating supplies Bryn had hauled up to his front door. "If I'd known, I'd have just met you at your place."

But Ailani was at her place. Maybe that was the safest answer, but Bryn wanted to be here with him. Exquisite torture she might regret tomorrow, but that was future Bryn's problem.

"Is this your way of saying you've never held a piping bag?" The flirty tone came so naturally around him. Was it even flirting if she was just being natural?

Another problem for future Bryn to ponder. Tonight she was just having fun.

"I don't even know what that is, Bryn." Nick set the bags on the floor, opened his apartment door and ushered her in.

Christmas music floated out of speakers. The tree they'd decorated was lit up in the corner. It still looked terrible, but he'd kept it.

"This is festive." And he'd done it for her. Nick wasn't into Christmas, at least not like Bryn. This was meant for her.

"Figured you'd like decorating to music. Though, if I'm wrong and this requires silence, then we can do that, too."

"This is perfect." She took the supplies to his kitchen, waited for him to set his stuff down, then opened the bag and pulled out a piping bag stuffed with green icing. "This is a piping bag, and it's going to be your best friend tonight."

"I kinda figured you'd be playing that role."

"I—" Words refused to trip from her tongue as she looked at him.

"But I can make friends with this, too." He winked and took the icing bag from her hand, setting it to the side. "I'm just glad you came."

"Why wouldn't I?" Bryn grabbed the box of sugar-cookie trees and put it on the table. "We'll start with these."

"Because of this afternoon."

"Please don't apologize again. Okay? I don't want an apology." The words were tighter than she'd meant them to be, but if he apologized again, she might spill all her emotions.

"But I am sorry. Sorry that our first kiss was rushed. That it was at the hospital. For an audience. I saw him, and it clicked who he was. And I couldn't stop my feet from moving to you."

"First kiss?" Bryn turned, her back against the table. She latched onto it with her hands. It was an awkward pose, but it steadied her.

"I've wanted to kiss you for days, Bryn. Since nearly the moment I laid eyes on you." Nick took a step toward her, then paused. "Maybe that isn't fair. I know this is supposed to be friendly—you helping me acclimate to Boston, and me supporting you as you step back into nursing."

Her eyes burned. It was all the right words. The ones she'd wanted to hear for so long. "Nick…"

"If you want to be friends, I can be that for you. I can. But I needed to say this. Needed you to hear, at least once, that my apology was for kissing you *at the hospital*. Not for kissing you. I'll never regret that."

"What if we call a mulligan?"

He stepped beside her, but she still didn't release the grip on the table.

"A do-over would be wicked good."

His *wicked* was still terrible, but she didn't care. Bryn released her hands and closed the distance between them. "Kiss me."

His hand rose, cupping her cheek. His eyes seemed to drink her in as his head slowly made its way toward her. The soft brush of his lips was the exact opposite of the possessiveness this afternoon. "Bryn."

Her name had never sounded like a worship before.

Pressing her lips to his, she pulled him as close as physically possible. She needed to know how he kissed, how he truly kissed.

"Nick, kiss me. Really kiss me."

The words broke whatever dam he'd been holding himself behind. His mouth claimed hers, and she melted into the moment, certain that there was no better place in the universe than being held in Nick's arms while his lips ravished hers.

His fingers skimmed her braid as her hands slipped down his hard stomach.

Finally, he broke the connection. Leaning his forehead against hers, they stood there just enjoying the heat and time together. It was magical.

"That was the best do-over ever." Bryn laughed at the silly words. "That sounded so dumb."

His thumb ran along her bottom lip, lightning sparking through the touch. "That was perfection. Plain and simple."

"We have dozens of cookies to decorate." Bryn pursed her lips as she looked at all the supplies she'd lugged up here. She'd promised to bring them in tomorrow.

Camp Heartlight was the perfect place for kids with heart conditions. It let them be themselves and let their parents give them an experience so many kids got without fear of the worst happening. Plus, Ailani knew she was here, so if they didn't bring in any cookies…

"Show me how to hold the piping bag."

"Was that a double entendre?" She giggled and playfully pushed at his shoulder.

His cheeks darkened. Though if she wasn't paying such close attention, she wasn't sure she'd notice. She put her hands on his cheeks, feeling the heat. "Was it, Nick?"

"No. Though that hasn't stopped my body from flooding with heat."

She knew better than to question that statement.

"All right—we ready?" She waited for a minute, then added, "For cookie decorating."

"I'm ready for whatever you want, Bryn."

She put the icing bag in his hand and pointed to the box of trees. "Those are yours."

"Yes, ma'am." Nick saluted and opened the box. "How do I do this?"

"It's really not that hard." Bryn grabbed the other green icing bag she'd made, outlined the cookie with royal icing, then filled it in, moving onto the next one while the first dried.

After doing six, she picked up the yellow icing, added a star at the top and lights. Finally, she grabbed the brown, outlined the trunk and held it up for Nick's examination. "See—easy."

"Sure." He laughed and pressed a kiss to her lips. "If you say so."

* * *

"Those look good."

"That's a lie, Bryn!" Nick dropped a kiss on her cheek. This evening was the definition of perfection. He'd kissed her, really kissed her, and the universe seemed to beat in rhythm with his heart.

The last few hours he'd kissed her freely. The only issue was that they were nearly done, which meant Bryn would leave soon. He wasn't ready for that.

"It's only because you're so stiff." Reaching her arms around his waist, she placed her hands over his and guided the bag of icing across the cookie.

"Relax."

How exactly was that supposed to be possible with her breasts pressed against his back? His body was hyperaware of every curve pressed against him. Cookies were the furthest thing from his mind.

"Nick."

"You can say *Relax* all you want, sweetheart. It's not happening when your body is pressed like that against mine. All I can think of is putting this icing bag down, turning and letting myself drown in your beauty."

"That is quite the line." She pulled back, and he set the bag down, reaching for her.

"Not a line." His fingers ached to undo her braid, to run through her long locks. To see them draped over his pillows. His mouth crushed hers.

Need, desire, it all blended into one with this woman. He'd always held himself back with women, not fully giving in to his wants. Bryn met each swipe of his tongue, each press of his hips against hers. She anchored him.

Kissing Bryn was nice, better than nice, but he craved so much more.

She pulled back, and he feared he'd gone too far. Let his ache escape.

"I need to text Ailani." She looked at the cookies, then at him.

"Of course."

Bryn held up her phone. "Should I ask if she can take care of Honey for another few hours, or…" She bit her bottom lip.

"Or?" He wanted her to stay. Wanted it desperately.

"Or should I ask her to take her out tomorrow morning, too?"

"I am always going to choose option B." Though if she was going to stay more often, he'd need to find out exactly what Honey needed. There was a pet store on the corner. Surely he could find everything there.

Or they could stay at her place, provided Ailani was all right with it.

Bryn's cheeks turned the most delectable shade of pink. She typed out a few things, then put her phone down.

"While we wait for an answer…we should finish assembling the cookie pouches."

Cookie pouches. He could focus on those… maybe. She'd made a promise, and he'd sworn to help her. "I still feel bad, putting one of your cookies in the pouch with mine. Yours are a work of art. Mine are…"

"Edible." Bryn's lips glided across his. "That's what matters, Nick. They're edible." Bryn turned, focusing on the cookie pouches.

"If you say so." He stepped behind her, wrapped an arm around her waist.

"You're right." Her words were thready.

He pressed his lips to her head. "Right?"

"It is hard to concentrate with you behind me." Her head leaned back, and he took the invitation of her mouth.

She tasted like sugar and holidays and everything he'd ever needed.

Her phone dinged, and he wanted to weep with relief as she moved to grab it.

Bryn laughed and shook her head.

"Can she walk Honey tomorrow?"

"Yes, she says, *Told you so.*"

"Told you so?" He reached for her hand, pulling her close as soon as her hand was in his.

"She told me she sees the way you look at me. That it was more than friendship in your eyes."

"Ailani is very observant." Nick ran his hand

along her back. At the hospital, he had to actively force himself not to look for her.

Bryn's eyes shifted to the cookie pouches behind him. "We still need to pack up the last dozen pouches."

He spun her so she was in front of the table, him directly behind her. "Nothing's stopping you," Nick pressed his body to her back, letting out a sigh as her butt rubbed against him with extreme deliberation.

His hands ran along her belly before dipping under the holiday sweater she wore. Her soft skin under his fingers was a waking dream.

"You are so beautiful." His lips feathered kisses along her neck.

Bryn let out a soft cry and moved her ass against him again. "Two can play this game."

"Good." He cupped her butt with one hand and let his other hand trail along the edge of her breasts. He was already hard. Already dangerously close to completion, and they'd not even discarded a single stitch of clothing. "I want nothing more than to spend the rest of this night turning each other on."

"All you have to do is look at me to turn me on."

Bryn's admission nearly turned his legs to jelly. This everyday woman whose mythical hold on him was so precious wanted him as much as he craved her.

"You're my own personal siren." He slid his

hand over her breast, rubbing the nipple through her bra.

"And you are doing an excellent job distracting me." Bryn leaned her head back, giving him perfect access to her incredible neck. "The quicker I finish these…" Her words caught as he slipped a finger into her bra.

"Or you could just say you have enough already. Three dozen, in fact. No one's going to fault you."

Her body tensed, but not in the way he wanted.

"Finish them, baby. It's fine. It gives me more time to find exactly what turns you on."

"Thank you for understanding." She kissed his cheek, then bent back over his table. The woman had been a people pleaser her entire life. With him, he wanted her to be herself. There was no way she could relax if she was worried about the cookies.

And Nick wanted Bryn relaxed as he explored every bit of her amazing body.

"Last one." She jiggled her butt again as she tied the ribbon.

He'd never considered himself such an ass man, but damn, the motion drove him mad.

"Finished!"

She turned in his arms, and Nick did not waste a single second. He lifted her, moving with as much speed as he could manage into his bedroom with her lips devouring his.

Laying her on the bed, he grunted, "Don't

move." He didn't wait for an answer as he moved to the bedside table and turned on the lamp. "I don't want to miss a thing."

Bryn slid to her knees and lifted her sweater over her head. Then she unhooked her bra. As he stood in front of her, she grabbed the edge of his shirt and ripped it over his head.

"My siren is demanding."

"You've spent the last twenty minutes touching me through my clothes and under them. Grabbing my butt and stroking my nipples. My body burns."

The words turned him on nearly as much as the sight of her perfect breasts.

Her hands skimmed over his stomach. "You are the hottest man I've ever seen."

"No one has ever said that to me." Nick lazily stroked her breasts, running a thumb over her nipples, enjoying the tightening bud.

"They were thinking it. They had to be." Bryn's mouth captured his, pulling him onto the bed.

"Bryn." His hand gripped her waist as her legs wrapped around him. They were still clothed from the waist down, and the urge to rip her pants down, claim her warred with the instinct to savor every moment, every touch.

Her hand reached between them, fingers flicking along his hardness. "Nick…" She nipped at his neck. "I need you inside me."

All thoughts exited his brain. She truly was

a siren. He pulled her pants and panties down together, dropping them on the floor without thinking.

"Your wish…" He trailed kisses along her breasts as he slid a finger inside her. "Is my command."

"Nick." Bryn's eyes widened as he stroked her inner core.

This wasn't what she'd meant, but her body moved against his hand, lost in the motion as she sought release.

He pressed his thumb to the top of her mound and couldn't stop the smile as he felt her tighten and let out a moan.

"You are perfection." Nick undid the buttons of his pants, slid them down and reached for the top drawer of his nightstand.

Bryn followed the motion and pulled the drawer open. She lifted the small gold package and carefully ripped it open, pulling the rubber out. Her green eyes held his as she cupped him and slid it down his length.

Her fingers skillfully caressed him before she guided him to her entrance. "Nick, I need you. All of you."

She wrapped her legs around him, and he lost himself in the haze with the beauty beneath him.

CHAPTER ELEVEN

"SWEET GIRL, you are so bouncy." Bryn laughed as Honey practically danced into the elevator. She felt the same excitement, but for different reasons. Nick was on shift this afternoon.

Not that she hadn't seen him every day since they'd decorated cookies. Two nights since he'd made her body sing. He saw her—the real Bryn—and liked her. It was intoxicating. She ached to wake next to him as she had after that night.

But that wasn't fair to Ailani. Honey was Bryn's responsibility. A responsibility she loved—Honey was family.

Ailani had casually mentioned before heading to the hospital this morning that she didn't mind Nick staying over. Bryn planned to take her up on the kind offer but ensure they didn't abuse Ailani's hospitality.

She didn't want to get her hopes up too much, but it was impossible not to when they felt like they belonged together. Like they were meant for each other.

It was a wild feeling to have, period, but after only knowing each other two weeks…

The elevator doors opened, and Kali was standing right outside. "Hi, Honey." She bent to pet the dog, then looked up at Bryn. "You look happy today."

"Do I?" Bryn felt like she'd had a perpetual smile on her lips since Nick had first kissed her.

"Yes." Kali winked. "Almost glowing."

A doctor walked up, looked at Honey and shook his head. "A golden retriever in a Santa sweater."

"This is Honey. Honey, Dylan." Kali beamed as she looked at the doctor.

When she turned to pet the dog again, Bryn noticed a similar look in Dylan's gaze. Romance seemed to be blooming on Ward 34…or her own happiness was putting romance goggles over her eyes.

"And I'm Bryn. It's nice to meet you, Dr. Geller." She knew of the visiting pediatrician but hadn't worked any shifts with him.

"You, too."

"I need to get to my next rounds. Life of a resident!" Kali smiled, but there was a hint of tiredness in her soul. Residents were too often overworked and exhausted.

"Take care of yourself, Kali." Dylan got the

words out before Bryn, but she was glad someone had said them.

Kali didn't say anything, but she raised her hand as she headed for the stairwell.

"I need to see a patient. Have a good day, Bryn, and very nice to meet you, Honey."

Honey wagged her tail as Dr. Geller walked away.

"All right, girl, you ready to see some patients and work your magic?"

Honey's deep brown eyes looked at her, and her tail wagged harder. Rationally, Bryn knew Honey couldn't understand the words, but it often felt like she did.

Stepping into the pediatric ward, Bryn was happy to see the all the holiday decorations. This unit was always brightly colored, but it still gave off *hospital* vibes—just *vibrantly painted hospital* vibes.

The tree, the pretend wrapped candy, the snowflakes the kids had made on the windows…it coated the feeling some. Though she knew the parents and patients would rather be anywhere else.

She and Honey walked to the nurses' station to check in. Instead of a nurse sitting in the main chair, there was a small child.

One not wearing hospital garb and coloring what looked like a worksheet from school.

"This is Mabel." Ailani strolled to the desk, and the little girl looked up and smiled.

"Nice to meet you, Mabel." Bryn smiled and offered the girl her hand for a high five.

Mabel hit it and let out a subdued laugh.

"Javi's babysitter fell through, so she's hanging at the nurses' station until her grandmother arrives." Ailani looked at the worksheet. "Looks like you've almost finished your homework."

"You don't look old enough for homework." Bryn laughed and looked at Ailani.

She shrugged in a way that made Bryn think she thought the same.

"Do you want to meet Honey?"

"Honey?" Mabel peeked over the desk and let out a squeal. "You have a dog!"

"She's a therapy dog. She visits with the patients to give them a smile."

"I'm not a patient." Mabel frowned.

"I know. But I need to look over the paperwork to see who wants to see Honey this afternoon. So you can keep her company while I look, all right?"

"I can do that." Her head bounced with the sincerity that Bryn found so heartwarming in children.

Somewhere between childhood and adult life, most humans lost the ability to just be themselves. Not to care about what others thought. She knew older individuals often rediscovered that trait, but that meant a lot of years not living authentically.

Something she'd done for far too long. A trap she still sometime felt like she wanted to slide back into.

"Do you have many patients today?" Ailani smiled over the counter, looking at Mabel.

"Not a lot, but I want to check on Logan first."

Her roommate looked up and pursed her lips, "His surgery went well, but his heart seems to hurt. Maybe Honey can help."

"I hope so." Bryn leaned over the desk. "Thank you so much for keeping Honey company, Mabel." The girl was rubbing Honey's ears and smiling.

Javi walked by the desk and looked over the counter.

"Careful, Javi. Someone will be asking you for a golden retriever soon."

His dark eyes cut to her, and he shook a head before looking at Ailani—a look that seemed to speak for itself.

"Come, Honey." Bryn snapped, and the dog dutifully stood and moved to stand by her. "All right, Miss Floofy, it's off to work for us."

"Bye, Honey!"

Bryn waved, laughing. This wasn't the first time—and it wouldn't be the last—that someone said hello or goodbye to the dog and not her.

She saw Nick step out of the staff break room and raised her hand.

"Nick!"

He turned. There was a look in his eyes—a sadness not hidden quickly enough.

"What's wrong?"

"Nothing."

Bryn tightened her hold on Honey's leash as she tried to adjust to the rough sound in his voice. "Nick, I can tell—"

"It *is* nothing. My father emailed. One meant for my siblings. I read it before he could recall it."

"Recall—"

"Yeah, recall. I got the notification while I was reading the invitation that he was recalling it. Trying to pull back what he'd sent. So…" He shrugged and blew out a breath. "Like I said. It's nothing."

That was a lie, but this wasn't the place for it. "Why don't you come to my place tonight? We can do dinner, then walk Honey and put on a movie. Just a nice, simple night."

"Sure." Nick nodded. "Though I hope I don't have to receive a bad email to get an invitation."

"Of course not. You're welcome anytime." Bryn reached out and squeezed his hand. "I'm off to see Logan."

"Good luck." Nick squeezed her hand back before dropping it. "His mom—" He paused, seeming to weigh his words. "She's not there, but it also feels like she is."

"The vibes are off. Got it." Bryn gave the leash the slightest tug as she and Honey headed to the room.

She knocked and waited for the permission to enter before heading in. Logan was in the bed, his leg up in traction with an external fixator keeping the pins in place. It was going to be a long road to recovery.

"You aren't wearing scrubs." Logan's eyes were sleepy, but he gave her a lopsided smile.

"I'm here today as a therapy-dog handler. You marked on your day sheet that you'd like an animal visit, if possible."

Logan laughed as he tried to lean over the bed.

"Nope. You stay there. She comes to you." Bryn held up a hand. There was a reason Logan was in traction. His leg needed to stay as still as possible.

"I hate being in this bed." Logan crossed his arms, but his smile grew larger as Honey stepped to the bed and put her paws on her the edge.

"I know. Staying still for so long must be hard, but Honey's here to release some of the boredom."

"I love dogs. I didn't do the paperwork—that was probably dad."

"Oh." Bryn kept the tone even. Kids talked more than adults, but teens were often hardened shells. Asking the wrong question could shut all communication down, so she'd gotten good at noncommittal phrases.

"He got a dog as soon as he moved out. A lab mix called Midnight. She is the cutest thing." Logan rubbed Honey's ears. "She'd be too excitable for the hospital, though."

"Honey has had a lot of training."

"Mom hates dogs. All animals, actually. I won't tell her you and I are best buds." He leaned his head against Honey's.

Bryn had no words for that. People might not like animals or could be allergic, but to hate them... Teens could be dramatic, but she suspected Logan watched his mother closely, trying to please a person who was unpleasable was a constant torture.

"What do you like doing? Skateboarding?"

"I did like it." He looked at his leg, his bottom lip wobbling before he focused all his attention on Honey. "Mom wants me to stop. She says this should be enough for me to focus on what's best for me."

What's best for us is Daddy staying home. You need to look pretty, be quiet, be sweet. Help me make him want to stay.

Her mother's voice echoed in her mind, but Bryn didn't know what to say. She'd spent her childhood trying to be what her mother had wanted. Trying to be perfect so her father would stay—something she knew now had had nothing to do with her. Her mother should have wanted what was best for Bryn, what made her happy.

It was such a low bar to get over, and it never stopped shocking her how many parents saw their kids as extensions of their wants and dreams.

"What do you want?" He'd had a serious injury. If giving up the sport was something he was thinking of, that was understandable.

"To get back out on the ramps." He glared at his foot. "I know it's dangerous, but so are other sports. I enjoy skateboarding."

"You're right. Other sports have injuries, too." She'd treated kids with injuries from soccer, football, gymnastics… There was a risk with everything. That was life.

"Sure. But other sports have college scholarships. They have respect. They make her…" Logan stopped and wiped a tear from his cheek.

In other words, his mother saw other sports as prestigious and skateboarding as a hobby that got her nothing. At least Nick had his father in his corner, but one loving parent didn't always make up for one unloving one.

"I just want to make her happy, and I never seem to do that. And now I'm in traction, and I have months of physical therapy, and she and dad are fighting, and—"

"And none of that is your fault." Words that

were so easy to say, but Bryn knew sometimes took a lifetime to fully accept.

"She's always unhappy with me, and I just think sometimes if I made her happy, maybe they'd figure it out." He sniffed and looked at the ceiling.

"I thought the same with my parents."

If I say the right things or love them better. If I make the house just like Ethan likes... People-pleasing was something she understood all too well.

"It really isn't your responsibility." Bryn snapped her fingers, and Honey hopped from the bed. "You are enough. Just the way you are."

"Doesn't always feel like it."

"I know." She shook her head. Broken bones healed—broken souls took much more work. "But when you doubt it, try to remind yourself. It's the best gift you can give yourself."

"Thanks." Logan's tone was one of a teenager, so sure they knew the world, sure they could find another way. She'd been that kid once, too. It was a lesson she hoped he learned sooner than she had.

"Will you bring Honey back?"

"I will. She'll be here in three days, and I will be back in scrubs tomorrow."

He closed his eyes, and she let the rest of the conversation she wanted to have float away. The teen had confided in her. That was a precious gift, and there was no telling if he'd do it again.

Stomping up the stairs to Bryn's apartment, Nick tried to push away the gloom cloud that had hovered over his head all day. But it persisted, reminding him over and over of the email.

His father was coming to Boston—for business, of course. After the new year, and he'd wanted to know what Nick's siblings thought of him stopping in to say hi to Nick. He'd said he figured he'd have a free night for dinner but didn't know if he should see Nick.

Then he'd made a joke about them all being busy serving on duty twenty-four hours. Before ceding that surely Nick kept himself busy, too.

Perhaps it was a joke, a bad one, meant for his siblings in uniform. He might've even pushed off the hurt if not for the *surely*. Like somehow them being forced to be on the clock twenty-four hours a day was a major flex.

Like most doctors, he worked twelve-hour shifts. It was exhausting and rewarding. And he loved it, so much more than he'd loved standing in uniform.

Something his father would never understand. Nick accepted that—even so, for his father to be so close and think of stopping in, ask his brothers and sister their thoughts and then recall it after he'd sent it...

Nick looked at his phone once more, wondering if his father might send a text or another email. Some acknowledgment that Nick had seen the email. Because he'd have gotten a notification that he couldn't recall the email. So he knew Nick had seen his words.

The silence ached.

The door to Bryn's apartment opened as he hit the top of the steps. "Honey could tell you were on your way." Bryn smiled, but he could see the worry in her eyes.

"Are you trying to tell me my footfalls are too heavy?" Nick chuckled, determined not to let his father's dig impact his night with her.

"It's an old building." She reached for his hands, pulling him into the apartment. The lights on the tree were lit, and the place smelled delicious.

She handed him a wine glass and opened the red. "You tell me when."

A heavy pour was what he wanted, but he didn't want to waste any time with Bryn while sloshed. "That's good."

"You sure?" She held the bottle up and raised a brow.

"Yes." He waited while she poured her glass, then clinked her glass with his. "My dad's email is bothering me."

She stood still, and he let out a breath and told her its contents.

When he was done, Nick waited for her to say something. Anything. Instead, she snapped her fingers, and Honey pressed herself against his legs as Bryn went to pull the salmon from the oven.

"Nothing to say?" He wasn't sure why that bothered him so much.

Bryn pursed her lips as she set the salmon on top of the oven. "When did you last talk to him?"

"It's been at least three years. A few months after mom passed."

She nodded. "Your choice, right?"

"I just got tired of him being disappointed in me."

"That's fair." She moved, wrapping her arms around him. "You're amazing. A fantastic doctor, kind, hardworking…"

"A great kisser." Nick dropped his lips to hers.

"Fishing for compliments." She pulled his head to hers, deepening the kiss, her body molding to his. A little slice of perfection in the difficult day.

"All right, Bryn. What's the 'but'?"

She pulled back, and he could see her weigh her thoughts. Moving back to the salmon, she grabbed two plates, quickly putting the fish and vegetables on one before passing it to him and walking to the small table.

She sat and took a deep breath. "I'm sorry he hurt you. That was unfair. But have you considered that he might want to see you?"

"See me?" Nick laughed. "My family was built on service,"

"You are serving, *Dr.* Walker. Just differently."

"Not according to my dad. You should have heard him when I left West Point. He couldn't even look at me. He graduated from West Point, my brothers and sister followed in his footsteps at West Point or other academies. I chose a different path, and that…"

"Nick—"

Now that the words were spewing forth, he couldn't seem to slow the flood. "He joked that I wasn't busy. Like somehow what I am doing is less important."

"Do you think what you're doing is less important?"

Nick's head popped back. "I…" Arguments formed in his mind. A loud *no* that he couldn't quite get out.

She reached her hand across the table. "Why are you hesitating?"

"I don't know." This should've been such a straightforward answer. A quick response.

"That's okay. But you didn't answer my question. Do you think he might want to see you?"

"He joked about me not being busy." Why couldn't Bryn see that?

"I know. The joke was in poor taste. But what if it alleviated the nervousness he felt? I'm not excusing that, but if he wants to see you, do you want to see him?"

Yes. His heart cried out at the idea. He wanted to see his dad. Wanted to know he was proud of him, though that wasn't something Nick thought was possible.

"You don't have to answer the question, Nick. Not to me, but you need to know the answer. You're an adult, you get to choose who you associate with, but maybe if you settled that part of your past, you might feel more comfortable staying in one place."

"Staying in one place?" He shook his head. "Bryn..."

"Just saying." She cleared her throat. "There's an ice cream shop around the corner. If you want an after-dinner treat, we can go there." She smiled, and he felt the air shift.

She'd pushed him, then backed off. The tough conversation wasn't done. His heart urged him to hash it out. Tell her that Boston was great, that he felt more at home here than he had anywhere else. But permanence wasn't really something he felt he did.

Heck, that was the argument his father had made when he'd left the academy. That he couldn't commit. That he was a quitter. Maybe his father had been right. He'd certainly left more positions than anyone he knew.

Bryn made him feel different, but that didn't mean the urge to move on, to go somewhere else wouldn't return.

"Ice cream sounds great."

"Perfect." Bryn grabbed her empty plate, but he waved her hand away when she reached for his.

"You cooked. It's only fair that I do dishes." He took her plate, letting his fingers trace her wrist before walking to the sink.

"I could get used to this." She grinned as she stood next to him.

Get used to this...

The words sent his heart racing. He wanted her to get used to this. She deserved it...but what if he let her down, like he'd let his family down?

"I'm going to hook Honey up." Bryn stood on her toes and kissed his cheek. "Ice cream in December. I'm so glad that you want a cold treat on winter day."

"Ice cream is good no matter the temperature."

"Agreed." She laughed and went to grab Honey's leash.

The easy conversation should've been nice. But it felt off, like she'd cut off a potential disagreement in midstream. He watched her hook up Honey and mentally pushed at the gloom cloud again. It wasn't as dark around Bryn, but it hadn't burst, either.

In fact, it felt more stuck in place than ever.

* * *

"Enjoying the milkshake?" Nick eyed her drink for the third time.

"Yes. Wishing you'd gotten a milkshake?"

"I think I chose okay." The man had stood over the counter for nearly five minutes before selecting regular chocolate ice cream. The Scooper hadn't hidden her smirk when he'd asked for a chocolate cone with chocolate ice cream.

"All those holiday flavors, and you choose chocolate." Bryn shook her head as he held the door to her apartment complex open. She was currently sipping a Christmas Cookie milkshake, enjoying the tiny pieces of cookie the blender hadn't quite crushed up.

It was an inane conversation. The same kind they'd had on the walk to the shop and back. The kind that kept them from diving back into her questions about his father's emails and the emotions it brought out in the man beside her.

The man she'd pushed further tonight than she'd pushed anyone in a long time. Her heart fluttered each time she remembered the hollow look on Nick's face as she'd asked him if he wanted to see his father.

She believed what she'd said. Blood connection didn't equate to family. But she also believed people could change. The email, and particularly recalling it, had been wrong. But his father had been asking about contacting him—it was a big deal.

And Nick wanted the connection. She could see it in his eyes. That didn't mean it was good for him, but he wanted it. Only he knew what that meant.

"I like chocolate. It's my favorite, and I got a fancy cone." Nick wrapped his arm around her as they walked to the stairwell.

"A waffle cone dipped in chocolate with chocolate ice cream. It's a lot of chocolate. Want to try the sugar-cookie milkshake?"

"How about I try it like this?" Nick used his free hand to put the keys into the door before dropping his head to hers.

His mouth ravished hers. The taste of chocolate on his tongue set her body ablaze. Like it had each time he'd kissed her, her body seemed to slide into his, her flesh aching to discard the barriers between them, just giving in to the desire.

"Bryn…" He said her name between kisses as he pushed her apartment door open.

She unhooked Honey's leash with one hand and snapped the command that send her to her crate. It was only after Nick lifted her into his arms that she looked over her shoulder to see if Ailani was there. No sight of her, so need to explain—though this needed very little explanation.

CHAPTER TWELVE

"THIS PLACE SCREAMS *BRYN*." Nick felt his eyes widen as she led him into the Christmas market. When she'd suggested this outing, he'd agreed because it made her happy. And making her happy was all Nick wanted, particularly because it felt like he'd misstepped the other night when she'd asked about his dad.

"I love it here. It's like holiday speed dating. There are so many independent stalls. The mixture of food and handmade gifts... There's something magical about the Christmas markets."

"So this is a yearly pilgrimage for you?"

"It was until Ethan and I got engaged. He was so weird about the holidays. Parties were fine, provided they were work colleagues, a way to schmooze his way to the top. Decor had to be picture ready."

"So you gave up something you loved because your fiancé... Sorry. Too personal."

"Is it?" Bryn frowned, then shook her head. She coughed and looked at her feet before saying, "Arguing about it was uncomfortable. So I just didn't."

Her quick shift last night about his dad popped into his brain. She'd shifted as soon as he'd gotten upset. Like she hadn't wanted to push him too far.

"Not overly proud of that choice, but it is what it is."

Nice going, Romeo. You've embarrassed the woman you care about.

Nick kissed the top of her head, trying to soothe the feeling that she was bending herself for him. That wasn't what he wanted, what he needed.

And dropping a question because your partner was uncomfortable was the opposite of cruel.

"So, what are we seeing first?" They followed the steps into the market, the holiday music blasting.

"The old ornaments. I always look for the original angel. I know the odds of finding it are super low." She laughed, but there was a hint of sadness in her tone. "But I always hope that someone will have it—and be willing to part with it for a price I'm willing to pay. You'd be shocked what the value of some ornaments are."

Except he wouldn't. Not anymore.

"Maybe we'll get lucky this year." He'd found this year's ornament and already wrapped it for her. She wasn't participating in the Secret Santa, but he planned to put it under the tree then anyway. And he'd set up an alert on several online sale sites for the original angel ornament—all with no luck so far.

However, the price tag on several ornaments had raised his eyebrow. Still, he'd paid a small fortune for the movies in his collection. What people prized was their choice, and he wasn't judging.

"Izzy!" Bryn raised a hand waving, then he saw her head back up. "And Dr. Murphy. I mean Ben. It's so nice to see you two."

"Bryn and Nick. Checking out the markets?" Izzy's smile was brilliant as she looked from her friend to Nick. The pediatrician was one of the sunniest people he knew, and that was saying something since he was standing next to a woman who practically radiated friendliness.

"It's Nick's first time." Bryn hit his hip with hers, then laid her head against his shoulder. "I worry it might overwhelm him."

It was such a couple action. Nick thought his heart might melt.

Izzy let out a chuckle, and Ben smiled.

At least Nick thought it was a smile. It was over so quickly.

"This place can be a bit much." Ben gestured to the gathered crowd as he seemed to pull into himself a bit.

"Don't worry, I'll keep you safe." Izzy kissed his cheek.

Ben cleared his throat and pulled a little away from her.

"I'll keep *you* safe, too." Bryn kissed Nick's cheek, her eyes moving from her friend to the uncomfortable-looking surgeon beside her.

"Well, it was good to see you guys." She squeezed Nick's hand.

"Have fun." Izzy waved before she and Ben wandered down the aisle toward a stall with holiday-themed children's items.

"Ornaments!" Bryn cheered, pulling him along.

"Ornaments." Nick dutifully followed, enjoying the sight of her giddiness. The music was loud, the place was crowded, food and holiday candle smells mixing in interesting ways. It was the definition of *overwhelming*, and watching Bryn love every minute was the best gift.

The booth they stopped at was overflowing. Even if her angel was here, he wasn't sure how'd they locate it. "All right." She held up her phone, the image of a tiny angel in a yellow dress sitting on a cloud in the forefront. "This is our mission."

Nick covered his mouth to keep the laughter from bubbling up. This meant a lot to Bryn, and he knew exactly what that angel looked like. Though he wasn't going to mention that. When he found it, he wanted it to be a surprise.

When.

The word clung to his heart as he started looking through his section of the booth. He'd always considered this an *if* project. If he found her angel. If he was still here. If…

Nick lived his life in *ifs*, not *whens*. Not absolutes.

Never absolutes.

A small heart ornament caught his eye. It was a red heart with the words Our First Christmas engraved over the center. The bottom of the heart had a little box where it said to write the year or names. A way to personalize it.

It was simple. Each year there were probably a few dozen ornaments produced like this for lovers. There was nothing special about it—until you added the names.

Nick needed it, wanted his and Bryn's names written on the bottom. The urge was so deep in his soul, it felt like if he didn't purchase it, he'd always regret it.

When. He wasn't sure when it had happened or how, but Bryn was his *when*.

Looking over his shoulder, he saw Bryn talking to the owner of the booth and showing her the image on the phone. He could tell by the movement of her shoulders that it wasn't good news.

He waited for her to finish her conversation with the woman, then opened his arms. "No luck?"

"She doesn't have it, but she knows someone that does. Seven hundred dollars." Bryn squeezed him, then stepped back. "No ornament is worth that."

He didn't agree. "I mean, that is a steep price, but you've been looking for so long. You could think of it as an investment."

"Nick." Bryn reached up on her tiptoes. "I want the ornament on my tree. Not in a box to stay precious with the hopes someone might pay me more for it. After all, it's only worth what someone will pay for it."

"We could ask for the contact. Maybe we could negotiate?"

"You're sweet." Her hand cupped his cheek as she shook her head. "But no. I'll keep looking. What's in your hand? Did you find an ornament? It's red. That matches your tree!"

Nick felt his mouth fall open. He hadn't even thought of that. The ornament matched the color scheme he'd inadvertently started.

She reached for it, her eyes widening as she looked at the box, then at him.

"It matches my tree, though that isn't why I want it." His cheeks blazed, and there was no way to blame the crowded Christmas market. Nick monitored Bryn's face, saw the tips of her lips move up and the corners crease on her eyes.

"Nick…"

"We should get it." He wanted it, and he wanted her to want it, too. Yes, their relationship was new. So new. But that didn't matter.

"These are meant for people that plan…" Her voice fell away as her thumb ran across the image on the box.

"Meant for people with more than one Christmas, right?" His voice was surprisingly steady as he asked the question. This moment was nothing and everything all at once. Nick knew what he was saying…what he was asking.

Her face stayed focused away from the ornament. He wasn't even sure she could describe it fully if asked. "Nick—"

"Bryn." He dropped a kiss on her forehead as she worked out what she wanted to say.

His heart hammered as he waited.

"Honestly…" She blew out a breath, her green eyes capturing his. "They're meant for people planning more than two holidays together."

A lifetime. All the holidays. The future. Home.

That was what these were supposed to mean.

He should put it back. They'd been dating less than a month. Yes, he was considering staying in Boston for more than a year…but that didn't mean forever. It just meant—

Nick didn't know what it meant. He'd never felt this before. Still, his brain screamed for him to find a funny joke, use laughter to escape the tension he'd created, but his heart seemed incapable of setting it down.

"I think we should get it." *We*—a word he'd never used in a relationship before—felt so perfect with her. When she said nothing, Nick continued, "As you pointed out, it goes with my tree."

"It does." Bryn's fingers brushed his as she looked at the ornament. It was a cheesy, but he wanted her to want it to. "Will it make you happy?"

It was a weird question, and he didn't quite know how to respond. *Yes* was the answer, but what if it didn't make her happy?

Bryn pleased people. She was stepping into her own power again. But he wanted this to please her, not an agreement to please him.

"I want it, Bryn, but not if it makes you uncomfortable. I know this is new and this ornament is a lot. It means—"

Her finger pushed against his lips, shushing his words. "I want the ornament, Nick." Then she kissed him.

In the bright light of the stall, with Bryn's arms around his neck, time seemed to stand still. Like the universe recognized what this moment was. What they were.

"Get a room!" The child's voice carried over the music, as did his mother's quick shushing noise.

Bryn burst into laughter as she pulled away, covering her mouth. "Maybe we should get the ornament and take the kid's advice."

Nick pulled her to him, dropping a soft kiss against her lips. "That sounds like the perfect plan."

* * *

"Stop pulling at the collar. You look fine!" Bryn smiled as she and Nick stepped up to the starting line for the Santa Dash. The Camp Heartlight fundraiser was well attended, which was good, but Nick might not have counted on so many people seeing him. Snow was likely on the way.

"Brr… Even in this outfit, I'm freezing." Bryn looked at the sky. Not a cloud in sight. But maybe, if it kept getting colder, they'd have a white Christmas after all.

"Nick!" Kali's bright call lit up behind them as the resident and Dylan pushed through the crowd to step next to them on the starting line. "I thought wearing Santa hats made us festive." She elbowed Dylan, then gestured to Nick.

"A full Santa suit." Dylan rubbed his gloved hands together, the tip of his nose already red in the wind.

Bryn squeezed Nick's hand as he fidgeted. The Santa suit had been her idea. Sort of.

She was wearing white pants, a frilly tutu and a snowman sweatshirt. Honey was in one of her sweaters and reindeer antlers. She'd mentioned wearing something festive to Nick, meaning a fun sweater or elf ears. Still, her heart had nearly exploded when she'd opened her door this morning.

It was clear he'd done it for her, to make her smile. It had worked! She was falling for him.

Who the hell was she kidding? She was tumbling headfirst in love with Nick Walker.

"You don't think it's too much?"

The Santa suit was perfect, but she knew he was hyperaware that no one else was in a Santa suit. He stood out!

In the best way possible.

"You should stop and see kids when we're done. I bet they'd love that." Ben rolled his shoulders as he joined the group at the starting line, his eyes focused straight ahead.

"Did I miss the memo on Santa hats?" Nick chuckled.

"Santa hats?" Ben touched his head and blinked as though he'd just remembered the hat. "Right. Uh. It was Izzy's idea."

"Where is Izzy?" Bryn looked at the crowd. So many faces in the mixture, though she suspected that if Izzy was running, she'd be by Ben.

"Not feeling up to a race this morning." Ben cleared his throat, his gaze still focused on the man holding the starting gun. "She's meeting me—us—at the finish line."

"Smart move." Nick jumped and blew into his hands. "If it's going to be this cold, it should at least be snowing! When are they blowing the starting gun?"

Honey barked, and he pointed to her. "She's ready to be warm, too!"

"She's ready to move." Bryn laughed and

reached up to drop a kiss on the tip of his nose. "There are a lot of people here, and she's very excited."

"Santa!"

A little boy pointed to Nick, and he bent and spoke to the child for a moment. The scene was enough to melt her heart.

"All right, I think Ben is right. We should stop by and say hi to the kiddos." Bryn thought Nick would enjoy the moment, too.

"I am usually right." Ben pulled one arm across his chest, then the other.

"Runners ready?" the race master called.

"Yes!" The chorus of cheers echoed across the gathered crowd.

"Is this a joke?" Nick jumped again, still trying to keep himself warm. "Of course we're ready!"

The starting gun sounded, and the crowd took off.

Dylan and Kali shot out of the gate. If they kept that speed they might not win, but they'd have nearly first choice of the doughnuts.

Ben hung with Nick, Bryn and Honey for about half a mile before he pulled away, too.

They were making a solid effort, but Bryn didn't want to push Honey too much.

"You don't have to stay with us." Honey could run the full 5K, but Nick was faster…and highly motivated to reach the warming tents set up in the hospital parking lot with hot cocoa and doughnuts.

"I know." Nick looked at Honey before focusing on the pavement. "But I've no plan to leave my best girls."

He was talking about the race. Bryn knew that. Nevertheless, her heart leapt at the words. For once, someone was staying in her life. He'd insisted on hanging the ornament on his tree. Front and center.

She glanced over at him, her whole body heating as she took in the Santa suit. She wasn't falling for him...she'd fallen. Head over heels in love with the man beside her.

"You make a pretty good Santa." Logan rubbed his hand over Honey's head. "Particularly with your reindeer." The teen's voice was high pitched, and Honey's tail wagged and wagged.

She would collapse once they made it back to the apartment, but for now, she was in doggy heaven.

"Pretty good?" Nick shook his head. "And to think I came with candy canes."

Bryn still wasn't sure where he'd found the bag, but it added to the fun as they visited the kid's rooms.

"Candy canes?" The teen rolled his eyes. It was playful enough, and Bryn was glad to see the interaction. Logan was moving from the hospital to a rehabilitation center in a few days. He'd not taken the news well.

Which Bryn understood. He wanted to go home, but that wasn't safe yet, something that was difficult for the teen to understand.

"All right, we have to head to the next patient's room." Nick passed Logan another candy cane. "Maybe they'll like my Santa outfit more." He winked and offered a wave.

"I appreciate it. I just like Honey more."

"Story of my life." Bryn laughed as the dog pulled her paws off Logan's bed.

They wandered out of the room, and Javi waved them over. "Can you stop in and see Jiyan? He's a four-year-old waiting for heart surgery and he's quite excited to see Santa."

Ailani walked up, and Bryn could see the worry on her face before she said anything. "Susie is being readmitted. The staff is transporting her from ER now. Maybe a visit from Santa will lighten the mood, if you don't mind another visit."

"Of course I'll see Susie." Nick's shoulders slumped, and Bryn wondered if her body language showed the same concern. Susie was meant to follow up with a cardiologist, though it could take weeks to get an appointment.

"We'll stop in after Jiyan." She blew out a breath and laid a hand on Honey's head, who sensed the tension and leaned her body against hers. "Good girl."

"All right, let's see Jiyan!"

Bryn followed Nick, hoping her smile looked good.

"Santa!" The little boy with dark hair clapped as he sat up in bed, a coloring book slipping from his lap.

His mother, Amita, leaned forward in her chair, smiling as she clapped in the same rhythm as her son. "It's Santa!"

"Hi, Jiyan."

The little boy looked at Nick, waved, then turned his attention to Honey. "Puppy!"

"And once more I'm outshone," Nick whispered as Honey walked over and did her magic.

"I'd say you get used to it, but…" Bryn made sure Jiyan didn't hear what she said—though, as usual, Honey was the star of this show.

Nick held up a candy cane and moved over to the bed to talk to Jiyan.

Bryn moved next to Amita, but the two of them said little while Nick and Honey worked.

After about ten minutes, Jiyan yawned, and Nick moved quickly. "Time for us to let you rest."

"But—"

"Rest is good, Jiyan." Amita's words were soft as she stood and pressed her lips to her son's forehead. "Tell Santa bye."

Jiyan smiled at Honey and waved at Nick

before lying back in the bed. "Bye, Santa and Honey."

"See, that time you got mentioned before Honey." Bryn chuckled, but she knew the sound was off. They were headed to see Susie. Anytime a patient was readmitted, it was difficult. But this was Susie's third admit in three weeks. And there was still no diagnosis.

"Time to see Susie." Nick pulled out two candy canes. "In case her mom wants one, too."

It was a good thought. The parents of chronically ill children were often exhausted. A candy cane wasn't much, but including Susie's mom meant a lot.

Nick knocked on the door and entered after Ellen called to come in.

Susie shifted in the bed, glaring at the cords monitoring her heart. Crossing her arms, she bit her lip, then turned her glare on Nick.

"I don't want to see Santa. Santa isn't real." Tears coated her eyes, and Ellen moved to her side.

"Susan—"

"It's fine." Nick looked to Bryn, passing her the candy canes. "I promise." Then he stepped out.

"That was rude, Susie." Ellen's scold was half-hearted, and she immediately dropped a kiss onto Susie's head. "I know you're upset about Daddy."

"If Santa was real, he'd bring Daddy home."

Susie let out a sob, and the heart monitors started going off. Her heartbeat was skyrocketing.

Javi, Ailani and Nick all stepped into the room.

The private rooms weren't that small, with equipment, patient, parent, and four medical professionals and a dog. It was nearly claustrophobic.

"Take a deep breath for me." Ailani's voice was calm as she moved past Bryn and Honey.

Javi looked at the dog and raised a brow.

Bryn gave Honey the order by snapping her fingers, and the dog immediately moved and jumped onto the end of the bed. She curled up tightly between Susie's legs.

"Focus on Honey." Javi's eyes were trained on the monitors, and Ailani coached Susie to breathe. Slowly, the child's heart rate started coming down.

"Good job, Honey." Javi checked the monitors one more time, then at Nick. "Can I talk to you for a moment, Santa?"

"That's not Santa."

"You're a very smart little girl." Nick took off his Santa hat and smiled at Susie. "After you, Dr. Pascal."

"Thank you, Dr. Walker."

The men filed out as Ailani checked the monitors on Susie's chest.

"I hate these." The words were soft and laced with tears.

"I know, honey." Ellen sat on the other side of

the bed and gently stroked her daughter's hair. "But we have to make sure you're okay."

"I want Daddy."

Pain hovered in Ellen's eyes, but her voice was strong as she said, "Me, too."

Ailani offered them a sympathetic look and held up the Call button. "If you need anything, just push this."

"Thank you." Ellen lay with Susie and Honey. She and Bryn sat in silence, and eventually the little one drifted off.

"Please tell Dr. Walker I'm sorry about Susie. She asked Santa to bring Daddy home last year and…" Ellen closed her eyes, a tear slipping down her cheek.

"But Santa couldn't deliver." Bryn finished the words.

"No one can. No one will even take my calls anymore."

Bryn and Nick had heard one side of this conversation the last time Susie had been admitted. Bryn hadn't wanted to push then, but it was clear that Susie's heart condition, whatever it was, was impacted by stress.

If there was any way to facilitate a call with her dad or something… Bryn would do her best to make that wish come true.

"Where is her dad?" Bryn slid into a chair while Honey snoozed with Susie. "You don't have to answer, but if we can help…" Her words died away, she wasn't even sure what she meant.

"I don't know."

Bryn pursed her lips. She'd seen that look on her mother's face so many times, not knowing where the man she loved was hurt her deeply. At least for Susie, it looked like Ellen was putting her daughter first.

Ellen sucked in a deep breath as she ran her hand over Susie's cheek. "She looks so much like Jack. Susie has his eyes and his nose. She looks so different now. He went on assignment thirteen months ago. Jack's an independent journalist. There was a hot story about a narco-terrorist on the island of Saloda. I didn't want him to go, but the pay…" Ellen wiped a tear from her cheek. "It was a lot."

Saloda had been in the news last year. Bryn hadn't paid much attention as she'd prepped for the wedding, but she'd seen a few reports. And suddenly the name Jack Cole clicked.

"Because it was so dangerous." She looked at Susie and recalled the news story of Ellen standing with a senator, begging for her husband's release from the narco unit—and the radio silence that had happened after.

"Always be wary of a deal that seems too good to be true." Ellen's laugh had no humor in it. "We got a proof of a life six months ago, but the news cycle has moved on. So my senators, both federal and state, have stopped taking my calls. The State Department says they're monitoring the situation, whatever the hell that means, and I have no contacts in the Department of Defense."

But Nick does.

"I just want someone to answer. I know the odds—I know the situation is dire and he might be gone forever. But I feel in my soul that he's still here. My heart swears it."

Maybe it did. There was so much about the human body that was still unknown, let alone the metaphysical world.

"And now Susie's heart condition… If Jack was here, he'd know what to do. We weren't able to get in to a see a pediatric cardiologist until the new year. Jack knows everyone—he probably even has some fancy contact from a story he ran years ago that could have squeezed her in. It's not fair, and our medical system needs a full over-haul, but I'd take it if I could get to know what is going on."

"I understand." Bryn knew better than most that the US healthcare system needed changes. Knowing that and also accepting that if you had a contact you'd use it for your child didn't make Ellen a bad person.

Bryn wasn't sure there was anything she could do, but maybe Nick knew someone. His family was rooted into the Defense Department. And his mother had worked for the State Department.

Susie was sick, but perhaps fate had dropped her at a hospital that could care for her physical self and her mental need for her father. Christmas was a magical time of year…maybe, just maybe, Bryn could grant this wish.

At the very least, she could ensure the hospital counselor talked to Susie and Ellen.

Standing, she rubbed Honey's head to get her attention. The dog stood slowly and gently stepped to the edge of the bed, where Bryn could lift her off without waking Susie.

"If I can help, I will."

Ellen offered Bryn a smile she knew meant *Thanks, but I doubt it.*

There was nothing left to say, so Bryn slipped from the room and ran directly into Ailani.

"Dr. Walker and Javi think they know what's wrong. Still need to talk to a cardiologist, but if she's in the early stages of aortic stenosis, the dizziness and fainting when stressed makes sense." Her smile was brilliant.

Bryn understood. Figuring out an unknown was a big deal.

Javi joined the small group, looking settled and at ease, certain that they were on the right track. It was reassuring, though she didn't see Nick.

Where is he?

"I've contacted Cardiology and Ben. Hopefully by Monday, we'll have an answer and a treatment path forward. Until then, we need to keep her as unstressed as possible."

Bryn looked at Ailani, then at Javi. What Ellen had told her wasn't in confidence, and Jack's detainment by the narco-terrorist group had made international news once upon a time. "I know why Ellen and Susie are so stressed…on top of the medical condition." She reached for Honey, running her hands along the dog's ears as she recounted what she'd learned.

"Wow." Ailani's face was devoid of color. "That's a lot."

"It is." But with Nick's connections, Ellen might get an answer, a contact who would at least return her phone calls. Bryn looked down the hall and still saw no sight of him.

"Last I saw him, he was in the break room." Ailani nodded in that direction. "Maybe grabbing some bake sale items after the run!"

"Probably." She needed to get to Nick. She wasn't sure why, but something felt off. He should've been out here. He and Javi had found a path forward for Susie, so why was he hiding in the break room?

Bryn headed over there, opening the door she called, "Nick?"

She moved the moment she saw the slump of his shoulders, pulling him into her arms. No questions, no recitation of what she'd learned.

"My dad's plans accelerated. He'll be in town

starting Wednesday. He emailed—again." He let out a bitter noise. "At least this one he didn't recall. Told me to reach out to his secretary to schedule a time."

Oof. Bryn didn't know the man, but telling your estranged son to contact you through your secretary wasn't the best look. "Do you want to reach out?"

Deep down she thought he did. He wanted what his father had given his siblings—acceptance. Bryn didn't know if that was possible, but if he never reached out, Nick would never know.

"No." He shook his head. "The man is here for work. I'm a side project, just like always. So no, I do *not* want to see him."

"All right." She loved him. If he didn't want to see his father, then he didn't have to. Though it made helping Susie and Ellen more difficult. She'd find a way—one that didn't upset the man she loved.

CHAPTER THIRTEEN

NICK FELL AND let out a grunt as his butt hit the ice…again.

"If you want to go, we can." Bryn skated around him as he brushed his hands against his knees. She'd tried helping him up the first few times he fell, but he'd unintentionally pulled her down with him and then spent the limited time he remained on his feet apologizing.

He'd wanted to see the Kelly Outdoor Rink. It was decorated for the holidays, and people were rushing around the rink. Or slipping and falling like Nick.

He slid to his knees, then managed to get back up onto his feet. "I don't think this is much of a date. Maybe it's time to move on."

"A new activity it is." Bryn looked at the rink exit. She could be there in three seconds, but Nick… "Do you think holding on to my arm will help you get to the wall and then the exit?"

"Absolutely not!" Nick shook his head, then

held his arms out as his feet started flailing. Somehow, he kept his balance.

He was probably right. She'd be just another impediment to his already slow movement. Still, not being able to help him was frustrating.

Bryn held her breath as they started the journey. Little kids whizzed past but avoided taking Nick out. By millimeters, they made it to the wall.

"I feel like I've won some award!"

She couldn't stop her chuckle. "The wall—great reward."

"Says the woman whose ass isn't freezing and aching."

Bryn kissed his cheek. "Poor baby. Why don't we go back to my place, and I'll take care of you." She winked as she skated backward. "Unless you're too sore?"

"Such a tease." He pulled himself along the wall. "If I was faster, I'd skate up, pull you into my arms and kiss away that playful smirk."

"That is very *Christmas movie* of you." She stepped out of the rink, then waited for him.

When he finally made it, she reached for his hands. "And you can always kiss me on unfrozen ground."

"Your wish." His lips were chilly as they met hers, but her body heated anyway.

"Bryn!"

Nick's hand wrapped around her waist as he

looked past her. She didn't need to follow his actions to know her ex-husband was behind her. Why he was calling her name when he could just pretend not to see her like he'd done so often in their marriage?

Still, she turned, appreciating Nick's arm sliding around her waist. Twice in one month after not seeing Ethan since the divorce was really too much.

His arm was wrapped around the waist of a blonde with green eyes. The man certainly had a type.

Ethan's date looked at him before looking at Bryn. "Umm… I'm Daisy."

"Bryn." She pointed. "This is Nick."

"Right." Daisy's gaze was hyper-focused on Bryn, never leaving her face.

"Well, we're just leaving. Have a good night." Bryn and Nick wobbled off to grab their shoes from their locker.

She waited for a moment before letting out the nervous chuckle she felt in her throat. "That was awkward for him, right?"

"I think he called your name by accident, then didn't know what to say." Nick shrugged as he pulled the skates off his feet and flexed his toes.

"Maybe." Bryn wasn't overly concerned with it.

"You ever think of moving? Then you'd never have to worry about awkward interactions again."

The question hit her heart, and she kept her

head down as she pretended to focus on tying her shoes.

"Bryn?"

There was an edge to Nick's voice. A point of pressure, like he was hoping she'd say yes.

Or I'm reading into things because I worry he'll move.

She'd given up her job at Brigham. It was hard to regret that because it had led her to the man beside her. But she wasn't leaving the place she'd always called home because her ex-husband resided in the same city.

"No." She pulled him to his feet. "Lots of people stay where their exes are. I'm not seeking him out but not running, either."

"It's not running. It's moving on."

Moving on. Was that how he thought of moving? And was it because he was restless or did something else happen?

"Why did you leave the last place you lived?" They'd talked of so many things but never what had led him to Boston.

"It just didn't fit anymore." Nick leaned his head onto hers. It was comfortable and easy, but it felt like he was trying to ground himself.

"But why?" If she knew, maybe she could sense the changes in him. Give herself a heads-up. The next time he moved on…if he asked her…maybe she'd go with him.

Boston was home, but maybe it could be somewhere else, too.

"I don't know. It just felt like time to move on."

"Just felt like it?"

"Yeah." He shrugged, like none of this was a big deal.

Maybe it isn't?

What happened when he felt the urge again? What might that mean for them?

Her phone buzzed, and she was grateful for the interruption. "Oh, it's an email from one of the state senators." She'd sent off a flurry of emails about Jack after her shift yesterday, hoping that another contact might yield results.

"It's a no, isn't it?"

"I haven't even read the…" Her voice died as she looked at the form letter telling her they appreciated her contacting them about this important issue and to be sure to remember to donate for reelection.

"Bryn."

"It's just the first contact. It's fine." She meant the words, but the sting of rejection still burned. Her gaze shifted to Nick, but his face was turned away. Once more, she swallowed the urge to ask him to reach out to his father. Nick had to cross that bridge.

Bryn's head was bent over her laptop as Honey laid her head in her lap. He watched her absently rub the dog's head as she scrolled through the internet, searching for contacts who might help Susie's dad.

Like Ellen hadn't exhausted every road.

Nick felt for the family. However, he also was realistic about the odds of getting Jack home soon. The quickest prisoner transfers took months. Many were yearslong endeavors with backdoor negotiations that only high-ranking diplomats ever knew about.

And that was when you were dealing with another government. Which the individuals holding Jack were not.

The US government had a standing rule that it did not deal with terrorists. At least not directly.

Bryn hadn't asked for his help. That stung. But he couldn't figure out why.

And even if Nick emailed, it didn't mean his father would help. The general made time for those who mattered—a tiny list that included his siblings, a handful of colleagues but not Nick. A lesson he didn't need to be reminded of.

His father's last email was a single line. No *Would love to see you*. No *Miss you*. No *Love you*. No *I'm proud*. He'd had emails from colleagues with more warmth.

Hell, even his father's assistant could have crafted a better message. If he'd let his assistant do it, then there might be more affection in the note.

Nick knew if it had contained microscopic evidence that his dad wanted to see him, he'd set up the time. Even if it meant asking his dad's assistant to "schedule" him in.

Was it too much to want his father to want him to stop by? To say that?

Bryn yawned, and he moved quickly.

"Take a break, sweetheart." She'd been at this for days.

"I will. In a few minutes." She reached for the coffee cup at her fingers, but he pulled it away.

"You need to rest. Adding caffeine at this hour—"

"Please!" Bryn giggled as she gently pulled the cup from his hand. "Are you really telling me that caffeine still affects you? How much did you drink as a resident? They live on the stuff, and so do nurses."

"Medical training abuses residents too often. That doesn't mean they should have to rely on caffeine to meet their ever-increasing workload. And nurses shouldn't need to, either."

"It's just coffee, Nick. I need to find—"

She was going to burn herself out. This wasn't sustainable. If by some miracle she found a way, this was a marathon, not a sprint.

"I'll pass it back if you can look me in the eye and swear that if it didn't offer you some sort of stimulant, you'd still drink it."

Her cheeks colored, and she opened her mouth,

then closed it. "I'm trying to help Ellen and Susie."

"Why?" The question popped out before he could catch it. He cared about his patients and their families, but this project was literally international.

"Other staff members grant wishes to the patients at Christmas. It isn't required, but I mean, think of this as me granting a wish for Susie and Ellen."

Nick knew his mouth was hanging open. What was he supposed to say to that? A wish! "Bryn—"

"I know it's a long shot."

"A long shot!" Nick shook his head. "Bryn, other staff members find a way for a person dressed as the kid's favorite superhero to surprise them. They get visits from the museum staff with items they can touch. Zoo animal visits. They do not facilitate international agreements! That would take a literal Christmas miracle."

"I know I won't get him home—I just want someone to tell Ellen and Susie they haven't been forgotten. Someone to notice that they're still waiting for the person they love. To pay attention to them. Is that so damn hard?"

"Yes."

She stood as his harsh word hit the room.

"Bryn, you have to be realistic. You can't please everyone and—"

"You think I'm being a people pleaser here? You think that's what this is?"

"Is it?"

She looked at her feet, then shifted on her heels. "No. It's trying to provide some relief to a parent who's been through more than she should have this year. It's about trying to bring a smile to a child who yelled at Santa to get out of her room." She let out a breath. "Nick, I might fail. I get that."

"Do you? Do you understand that you might not be able to bring anything to the table here? Sometimes you have to just move on."

"I don't *move on*." Her whole body seemed to shake as she stared at him. "When I care about something, about someone, I don't move on."

They were dangerously close to talking about something other than Ellen and Susie.

Pulling at the back of his head, Nick tried again. "You don't know anyone who can help."

"Not true." She closed her eyes, her bottom lip shaking, before she straightened her shoulders and looked at him. Her green eyes said the words before her mouth could.

"Bryn."

"I know you. And *you* know someone. Your family has connections."

Connections. There it was. The fact that his family had access to a part of the world almost no one else did. His family, but not Nick.

He got recalled emails and one-line statements telling him where his father would be. Nothing that let Nick call in this kind of favor. Was that why Bryn hadn't asked him to help?

Was that why she'd waited until they were arguing to even bring it up? "And yet you didn't ask me, did you?"

Bryn shook her head, and for the first time in their short relationship, she didn't quite meet his gaze. It was the same action his father had taken when Nick had explained he wasn't returning to West Point. Looked past him.

"Would you have reached out? Will you?" Bryn sounded too hopeful.

"No." Nick hated how fast the word slipped from his mouth.

Seeing his father, asking him for a favor…one he probably wouldn't be able to grant. Assuming he was even interested in trying.

"All right."

Her soft answer sent shock waves through him. Where was her anger?

"All right? Just 'all right'?"

The lines around her eyes deepened, and he hated the frown on her face.

"Yes. Just 'all right.' You get to decide what you need from your family. I can't make that choice for you."

Nick's chest ached as she turned back to the computer. The slump in her shoulders gave away her disappointment, but she didn't argue. She was giving in—just like she'd done with her ex-husband. Reading him and giving him what she thought would make the situation go away.

"My father might have access to someone. At the very least, he could probably pull a string to get a senator's aid to return a call." He didn't know why he was doubling down here. She'd let him off the hook—he needed to drop this.

"Given what I've learned regarding the joint chief of staff, the Department of Defense and the group holding Jack, probably." Bryn grabbed the coffee mug, tipped it up, finishing it before she started typing again.

A freight train seemed to blow through his mind. What was happening? "So you aren't mad at me for not reaching out?"

Bryn shook her head but didn't look at him.

"I think you're lying. I think you're angry and you're trying to please me like you did Ethan." He was not her ex-husband. He cared about her. Full stop.

He wanted Bryn—all of her. The fun, joyful woman who brought him so much life, but also the tough woman. The anger, the sadness. Those emotions were part of life, and he didn't want her hiding them.

"Do you want me to be angry?" Bryn rubbed a hand over her forehead before she looked at him. "Do you want me to make you see your father? I'm your girlfriend, not your mother or your counselor."

"I want to know your actual thoughts. I want the words you're holding back. What do we have if you aren't honest with me?"

"I can't help you with this. Until you realize that your achievements are worthy no matter what your father thinks."

"I am not looking for my father's approval."

"Yes, you are. Whether you're lying to me or yourself right now, I don't know. But you want it."

"I don't need him. He turned his back on me. I graduated from med school, and he didn't even come. If a success doesn't happen in uniform, it doesn't matter." Nick's hands were shaking as he looked for his keys. He needed to leave before he said something worse.

"You asked me for honesty. You wanted the words. You can't get upset with me for giving them." Tears hovered in her eyes, but they didn't spill over. This was the woman who'd found herself again after her husband had turned from her on her honeymoon.

The strong woman he'd fallen in love with her.

"What are you looking for?"

"My keys."

They hit his chest a moment later.

"Bryn…" Her name on his lips nearly broke him as he grabbed the keys from the floor.

"I wasn't trying to please you. I was trying

to protect you." A tear slipped down her cheek. "And now you're running."

"I'm not running."

"Then why the keys, Nick? This is our first fight. They happen between people who…" Her fist pulled to her chest as she sucked in a deep breath. "Who care for each other. If you run now, will you ever stop?"

The room's walls were closing in, the air thickening. His mind refused to listen to his heart's command to stay. To tell her it wasn't her he was running from. To explain that he didn't even know what it was pushing him toward the door. But he needed to leave.

"I need time."

"Time? Nick…"

"I'm sorry." His emotions were all out of whack. It felt like the shell around his soul was cracking. And he didn't know if anyone would like what was underneath.

He was in his car, sitting behind the wheel with no memory of exiting the apartment or running down the stairwell, when his final words echoed in his brain.

Had he told her goodbye? Kissed her cheek? Given any indication that he'd meant he needed time tonight?

Did I just break up with her?

Leaning his head against the steering wheel, he let out a soft sob. His soul urged him to go back upstairs, apologize, make her understand that he didn't need his father's acceptance.

Except what if she was right?

She wasn't. The fear, the sadness—none of it was tied to that. He was going home. Getting a bit of sleep, putting himself back together.

He'd call her first thing. Ask her for coffee. Put everything to rights. It would be fine. It would.

CHAPTER FOURTEEN

"WHERE'S HONEY?"

Susie's frown didn't bother Bryn as she stepped into the room. She wasn't the first patient—and she wouldn't be the last—to look a little sad when Bryn didn't walk into a room with the ball of fluff beside her. "She's at home."

Holding up the stethoscope, she smiled, though her heart wasn't really in the motion. "I'm your nurse today."

"And you want to check my heart?" Susie rolled her eyes, then looked to her mother.

Ellen was giving her the look all moms seemed to develop. It said *Behave.*

"Everyone is listening, checking your heart, aren't they?" Children picked up on so much more than adults gave them credit for. And children who spent time in the hospital seemed to grow up even faster.

"Everyone." Susie lay back and adjusted the lines of the monitors on her chest like a pro. "I hate these."

"That's normal." Bryn moved to the side of the bed. Her job this morning was to make sure the electrodes monitoring for any decline or acceleration of Susie's heartbeat were properly attached.

The door opened, and Nick stepped in with Dr. Jarod Keegan, an interventional cardiologist.

Bryn saw Ellen sit up straight, her hands grasping the edge of the chair that she'd rarely left over the last few days. Two doctors.

She knew Javi had explained the aortic stenosis, commonly called AS, the diagnosis they were scoping out. And Ben had consulted, too. That it was Dr. Keegan here and not Ben was an actually a good sign.

Dr. Keegan had completed his schooling at Howard University. The black man's hair was graying at the temples, but he was one of the top cardiologists in the country. And if he was here, it meant open-heart surgery wasn't necessary.

Nick's eyes stayed focused on Ellen, away from the bed where Susie was. Away from Bryn. Silence from the man she loved could be the loudest sound in the world.

"Ellen, I want to introduce Dr. Keegan. He's an interventional cardiologist."

"I know the polite thing is to say *Nice to meet you, Dr. Keegan*, but…" Ellen looked at Susie and then the two men before her.

"But it's not." Dr. Keegan nodded. "I know.

Trust me, you aren't hurting my feelings by acknowledging that you'd rather be anywhere else."

"Another doctor?" Susie bit her lip and pulled a small stuffed animal to her chest.

"Yes." Dr. Keegan moved toward her. "I'm here to talk to you and your mom about what we have to do to help your heart."

"An interventional cardiologist—what does that mean?" Ellen's foot was tapping, her eyes laser focused on the cardiologist.

"The echocardiogram confirmed Dr. Walker and Dr. Pascal's suspicion of aortic stenosis." Dr. Keegan looked at Susie and explained, "Remember when the nice lady with the big machine came in here and used a wand on your chest to see your heart?"

She nodded.

"Well, that showed that one of your heart valves isn't as big as it needs to be. So we're going to put a balloon in your heart to widen it."

"Will it hurt?"

"No. You'll be asleep, and when you wake up, your mommy will be there."

While Dr. Keegan was comforting Susie, answering all her questions, Bryn looked at Nick. The man had been silent this whole time. Which made sense, if she was honest. He was here as Susie's pediatrician of record during this shift. This was Dr. Keegan's show. But she wanted to hear his voice.

She'd started so many texts, pulled up his number at least a dozen times since he'd walked out of her and Ailani's place two days ago. And she'd not followed through with any of them.

I need time.

She didn't know what that meant. But she wasn't going to push him. She'd adjusted herself for Ethan. Molded herself into a model for him. She wasn't doing that again.

She was looking for ways to help Ellen. Maybe she wouldn't be able to, but she wanted to help. And it wasn't people-pleasing because Ellen hadn't asked and didn't even know.

Bryn knew what it was like to feel forgotten. If she could help Susie and Ellen avoid that, particularly around the holidays, there was no stopping her.

"If you have questions, let me know. I've got the OR scheduled for the twenty-third. We'll let Santa know you'll be home a few days after Christmas."

"He's not real." Susie's tone was just as strong as it had been when she'd made the comment to Nick after the Santa Dash.

So young and disheartened.

Dr. Keegan didn't argue, he just patted Susie's leg. "You'll be home in time to enjoy watching the New Year's Eve fireworks."

Susie nodded but didn't say anything else.

Dr. Keegan headed out, and Ellen looked at Nick. "Is there anything I should have asked?"

"No. You did great." They were the right words, said in the right tone, but his bedside manner was lacking.

Was that because she was standing here?

A year ago, maybe even a few months ago, she'd have ensured that it wasn't her. Hell, she'd left Brigham to please her ex-husband! She wouldn't be doing the same here. Ward 34 was her place.

But she was also worried about Nick.

"If you need anything, please let me know, sweetie, all right?" Bryn squeezed Susie's hand and then walked out.

She hovered outside of the door. Nick stepped out and nodded, his brown eyes not quite meeting hers.

"Nick…"

All her words seemed locked deep inside. "Are you going to the staff holiday party this evening?"

"I'd planned to."

Bryn waited, but he didn't say anything else. "Nick—"

"Dr. Walker!" Leigh Wachowski, the head nurse, waved a hand, "Teen in room six can't stop throwing up. I think we need to start IVs to prevent dehydration. Can you take a look and write up the order if you agree?"

"Of course. Have a good day, Bryn."

Have a good day. On the outside, they were nice words. Friendly words between colleagues.

If she'd had any doubt that he'd meant *time* as a reference for a breakup, this shattered the illusion.

People walked past her in the hall. She registered their presence but little else. Her heart still beat, even though her soul swore it shattered. Life moved on. She wasn't sure how she was going to do that, but that was a question to answer in a few hours. Or a few days.

Today she'd do her best not to be alone with Nick. And she'd skip the holiday party. Ailani could bring along the cookies she'd made for the party.

But that was the simple answer. The safe answer. It was also the route she'd taken at Brigham. Stepping aside so Ethan had his place.

She and Nick could coexist here. Or he could move on. Her broken heart nearly collapsed at the thought of him leaving. Eventually he'd leave. Find another place. A new adventure. Away from her.

This was her place. Which meant sticking around. Going to the party. Putting on a happy face. She could do this. Somehow.

"Bryn." Izzy smiled as she passed over a tablet chart. "Can you start meds on my patient in room two?"

"Yes." She took the tablet chart, but before she could turn, Izzy's hand was on her shoulder.

"Are you all right?"

"Fine." The word women had used for generations to mean *no* but say *yes*.

Izzy squeezed her hand. "If you need to talk, I'm here."

"Thanks." Bryn tapped the chart in her hands. "Let me take care of your patient."

"Just remember to take care of yourself, too."

Holiday music blasted from the staff speakers. Paper snowflakes were hung on the windows, and the Christmas spirit seemed to fill everyone except for Nick. He placed the small present for Bryn and the envelope with his Secret Santa gift under the tree with the other gifts. The tree had giant red balls and blinking lights, and the array of boxes underneath it was impressive. Which made his small envelope for Secret Santa look a little sad.

He'd drawn Liz, a radiology tech, who, according to the intel he'd received, loved coffee. So he'd gotten a gift card to Full of Beans. It was a fine gift. One that would make the radiology tech smile. It wasn't deep, though. Not personal.

Not like the small box he'd just laid under the tree wrapped in paper covered with brightly colored Christmas trees. An inside joke about his tree. The gift he'd hoped to share with Bryn following her shift on Christmas morning. A dream that wouldn't come true now that they weren't speaking.

Nope, the gift he'd found, the one he was so proud of, was going with the other Secret Santa gifts. At least she'd have it, though. That was what mattered.

He'd thoroughly messed all this up.

His plan to call her the next morning had fizzled in a ball of nerves. He'd always joked that movies made too much out of the hero and heroine not talking, called it unrealistic.

He'd wanted to believe he was immune to such things. As days of silence had grown between him and Bryn, he'd realized how human it was.

The real pain was knowing there was an easy way to fix it. Call his dad. Get the contact.

Easy…

"Bryn."

He heard Izzy's bright voice saying her name, and his head turned. Bryn wore a green sweater, brown pants and a star headband. She looked professional and like a Christmas tree. A look only the woman he loved could have pulled off.

Loved.

He loved her. And now he was standing on the opposite side of a holiday party with no idea how to bridge the cavern he'd dug between them.

"Look at these cookies!" Izzy held up what looked like the cookie Bryn had talked about making for tonight. Not as fancy as the ones she'd made for the bake sale, but much better than the ones he'd tried to decorate back when he still could.

"I think we might have too many sweets." Bryn's laugher made his heart sing, while it sent shards through his soul.

He shouldn't be here. Except the only place he saw Bryn now was on Ward 34. It was bliss and torment wrapped into one.

"It finally snowed." Ailani's voice was soft as she stepped next to him.

"It did." Nick had waited the entire month to see snow. Bryn had told him Boston rarely had a white Christmas. Today he should've been throwing snowballs at her, watching Honey roll in the wet stuff while Bryn playfully scolded her.

"You doing all right?"

There was no succinct answer to Ailani's question. *No* might be a complete sentence, but it was so much deeper than that.

"Fine." He crossed his arms, then uncrossed them, then crossed them again.

"You certainly seem fine," Ailani murmured, her eyes focused on the thick snowflakes falling outside.

He wanted to ask how Bryn was. Except he wasn't sure there wasn't a non-creepy way to do it.

If she was all right, if the laughter he'd heard a

minute ago was real, that was a good thing. But it also meant she was fine and he…well, he very much wasn't.

"Bryn says she's fine, too. It's like you guys are running off the same script."

Ailani waited a minute, then wandered off.

Nick counted snowflakes, giving himself to the count of fifty before he had to turn around and put on a cheerful face. Or a happy enough face.

His phone buzzed, giving him one more reason to ignore the general holiday feeling around.

Pulling the phone from his back pocket, Nick felt his heart drop at the email.

Something came up—in town until the day after Christmas.

Another one liner with no personal message. At least the general was consistent.

"Time for Secret Santa!"

The peppy call came up, and Nick instantly regretted putting the present under the tree. He needed to step out. Just for a moment.

He swore when he came back, he'd be as jolly as St. Nick. Somehow.

"Happy holidays." Kali held up one of the holiday paper cups from the punch table.

"Happy holidays." Bryn raised her own cup,

ensuring her eyes never strayed to the window where Nick seemed to be camped out.

"And it's snowing!" Kali pointed to the window.

"It is." She tried to sound happy. A white Christmas was truly magical. And Nick had wanted it. Was he excited?

"Delivery for you, Bryn." Leigh gave her a small box.

"I didn't do Secret Santa." She passed it back. It was a fun tradition, one she would absolutely take part in next year.

But she hadn't been a full employee and hadn't been in the holiday spirit when she'd seen the signup.

Leigh shrugged and handed it back. "It has your name."

Pink, blue and green trees covered the paper. Her eyes filled with tears as she rubbed her fingers over the images. It wasn't pretty paper. It was pretty horrid. And she loved the hidden meaning behind it.

A hidden meaning that meant she knew just who had left her the present. A present from Nick, under the staff tree. Not under his tree. Not under hers.

"Are you going to open it?" Kali was all grins.

"No."

Kali blinked and gripped her wrist. "Bryn…"

"Just going to wait until I get home. I…umm… I didn't get a gift for anyone else, so…"

"I didn't, either." Kali nodded, but Bryn could tell the resident knew she wasn't being quite honest. "I think I'm going to check on Dylan again. Jiyan's still in surgery."

"Right." She blew out a breath and slid the small box into her purse. Tonight she'd open Nick's present. And grieve the second message that seemed to call from the gift.

Goodbye.

CHAPTER FIFTEEN

"BRYN, DO YOU have any acetaminophen? My feet are aching, and I still have another six hours on this shift."

Bryn peeked over the fridge door as Izzy leaned against the locker bank. "If you open locker fourteen, my bag is in there. I have acetaminophen, or if your feet are aching, you can grab the ibuprofen." Ibuprofen was better for aches and pains, but as a physician, Izzy knew that.

"Acetaminophen will work."

"Izzy?" Bryn's mental radar raced. She'd been feeling under the weather, not drinking…and now avoiding ibuprofen.

Could Izzy be expecting? Before Bryn could travel too far down that mental road, Izzy held up the small angel ornament. "This is so cute."

The little angel was wearing a yellow dress, sitting on a cloud with her eyes closed. The first in the series. Nick's gift for her. It was the sweetest gift she'd ever received. Something she'd tell him, if she ever saw him.

It was strange. After seeing each other every day for several weeks, it was like he'd poofed out of existence. She saw his names on charts, but since the staff party, she hadn't actually worked a shift with him or laid eyes on him.

"It's the first in a series for the ornaments I collect."

Izzy's eyes widened as she looked at the ornament. "Really? Why is it in your purse?"

That was an excellent question. One she didn't really have an answer for. Nick's gift should've been on her tree. Or packed away where she didn't have to see it every day. Instead, she was carting it around like a comfort item.

A comfort item from the man she loved but hadn't seen or talked to in days.

"Nick gave it to me." Bryn bit her lip and squeezed her eyes closed, refusing to allow the tears to fall.

"I see." Izzy's voice was quiet, but Bryn felt her arms slide around her shoulders, squeezing them tightly.

Her lovesick pain was probably very obvious to everyone.

"I'm all right." She had told Ailani the same thing when she'd asked. And Izzy's look was so similar to her roommate's that she knew her words weren't convincing.

"What happened?" Izzy grabbed a bottle of water and downed the two pills before sitting back on the bench.

"I don't know." How dumb did that sound? Things had been fine, and then they'd been arguing and he'd walked out. "Nick's father is in town. He's reached out a few times, but Nick isn't interested in connecting. I did my best to give him space on that, but then it was almost like he got mad at me for doing that. It was so hard to read."

"Hard to read?" Izzy's brows rose. "Do you read people often?"

"Of course." Bryn shrugged as she peeled the banana she'd grabbed from her lunch bag. Medical staff rarely had time for a full break, but she kept easy to grab snacks in the fridge.

"Of course…" Izzy flexed her feet, then added, "You realize not everyone does that, right?"

"Does what?"

"Reads people's emotions."

"Yes, they do." How could one interact with others if they weren't gauging their reactions? Understanding how things might affect them… pleasing them.

Bryn rubbed her hand over her brow. She'd grown up with an inconsistent mother. Always trying to game how she might handle a situation. And she'd done her best to be what Ethan had wanted…doing the same thing.

Izzy pulled the pager from her hip and looked

at the numbers. "I'm sure reading people has its uses."

But it also kept her from fulling connecting, let Bryn hold back rather than fully embrace others. Rather than tell Nick she'd like his help or explain that it would be nice if he reached out to his father or gave her the contact, she'd held back.

Intent on making sure he wasn't uncomfortable.

Guessing that asking him would upset him. But upsets happened. That was life.

"I need to see a patient." Izzy rotated her feet one more time before standing. "If you need something, you'll let me know?"

"I feel like it's me that should say that." Bryn winked as Izzy's cheeks colored before she headed out the door.

Bryn lifted the angel and gently placed it back in the locker. When her shift was done, she was texting Nick. It was time they had a conversation. If it didn't go the way she wanted, well, she'd deal with that when she had to.

"It's Christmas Eve. Please. I just want to know my husband hasn't been forgotten." Ellen's voice shook as she leaned against the wall of the garage. The same place he and Bryn had seen her weeks ago. Fighting the same battle.

"Ellen?"

"Oh, Dr. Walker." She let out a soft sigh. "I

stepped out for a few minutes while Susie was resting. She came out of surgery yesterday. It was successful, but she's still tired."

"She will be tired for a few days. It wasn't open-heart surgery, but it still takes a lot out of a little body." Nick moved to stand beside her on the wall. "But you don't not have to feel bad about stepping out here to check on your husband."

"'Checking.' More like 'screaming into a void.'" Ellen kicked at a rock. "Nothing feels right with him gone. The world is a little darker, the music a little dimmer. Jack—Jack is my home, and for the last year no one, except Bryn, has even given me the time to listen to our story."

Bryn.

"I mean, she can't even do anything, but she listened and even called a few senators."

She'd done more than that. He'd watched her search everything she could. He could only imagine what she'd done in the days since he'd left.

"She's a special person." The description didn't come close to describing the woman he loved. The woman he'd accused of people-pleasing, when she was the one who'd seen what Ellen and Susie really needed—someone to notice them. And he'd let his own issues with his father get in the way.

"I need to get back to Susie. Thanks for chatting for a minute."

Nick raised his hand as she stepped back into

the hospital. He looked toward the rows of parked cars, then pulled the phone from his pocket.

He blew out a breath, then pulled up the text he'd gotten from Bryn.

Can we talk?

Three little words that sent a rainbow of emotion through his body. His fingers hovered over the digital letters before he backed out of the texts. There was something he needed to do first.

So he pulled up the number he hadn't reached out to for years.

If you're available, I'd like to talk.

Nick put the phone back into his pocket, and then it vibrated. It couldn't be his father. He never got back to people this fast—or rather, he didn't get back to Nick this fast.

Still at the office. Will be here a while.

Working. In the local field office. On Christmas Eve. Technically, Nick was working, too, but at the hospital. It was different.

Before he could type out a fine or think of a way to ask for a favor via text, his father texted again.

This time it was an address.

It was probably as close as he was going to get to an invitation. So he should take it.

On my way.

The office building was like so many around Boston, though it lacked any company names on the walls and there were more than a dozen cars in the parking lot long after hours on Christmas Eve. The formidable-looking security guard sitting behind the desk didn't look pleased to see him. He'd been in enough places like this as a kid to recognize the signs.

Secure building. One he didn't have clearance to enter.

Here.

His father had likely been notified the moment he'd stepped through the door, but the text at least gave him something to do while the guard sized him up.

"Let him in."

Nick's heart nearly split in half as it tried to decide if it was excited or terrified to hear his father's voice over the guard's radio. There was still time to turn around.

But Bryn needed him to follow through for Ellen and Susie. So his feet moved forward.

"He hasn't even shown any ID. And he isn't on security's list for tonight." The guard didn't take his eyes off Nick. His left hand held the walkie-talkie, the right hovered close enough to his waistband to draw the weapon in the holster.

An entry list for Christmas Eve. How very Dad.

"I'm aware, Tristan. I said let him up."

"Fifth floor?"

"Third."

So whatever "party" was going on was happening on the fifth floor. Some late-night secret operation? Probably. Did his siblings know?

Maybe. Though if they did, they wouldn't be able to tell him, either.

Nick swallowed, trying to force the weight of unworthiness down. He was here for Bryn. For Ellen and Susie.

He wasn't a quitter.

Tristan didn't bother to say anything as he walked to the elevator, punched a set of numbers into the keypad and stepped back.

Nick slid into the elevator, the *3* already lit up. Pushing the other buttons would have no effect, but Tristan pointed to them anyway.

"You go to three and then right back here."

Nick barely resisted the urge to offer him a salute as the doors closed.

Not like it's my fault my father is in charge of whatever is happening here tonight.

When the doors opened on the third floor, Nick pushed himself off the back wall of the elevator, then gave a little wave to the camera in the corner.

The long hallway had four doors, and only one was open. Apparently meeting the son he hadn't seen in over ten years in a place other than an office building wasn't an option his father was choosing. Fine.

Walking through the open door, Nick paused, taking in the general behind the desk. The man wore civilian clothes now. The touch of gray at his temples had taken over his father's entire head. He looked somehow smaller than the man in Nick's memories.

"Seems like you have a lot going on tonight." Maybe that wasn't the best way to address his father for the first time, but nothing more traditional seemed to want to make its way out.

"Christmas Party."

Nick raised a brow but didn't call out the lie. Even the Department of Defense didn't usually work on Christmas Eve.

"So, what do you need?"

Right to the point. He wanted to call his father's bluff, wanted to point out that his father had sent the first email. And let him know he was staying in town longer. Nick hadn't initiated this.

Unfortunately, he was right. Nick was here for a favor.

"I need you to ask a senator or someone with connections about a man named Jack Cole." He knew those words were off, but he didn't know who exactly his father needed to ask. "And have someone call his wife, Ellen."

"Jack Cole? The journalist taken captive by the narcos?"

"You know the case?" His father was well connected, but even he couldn't know everything. Nick had expected his father to ask a few questions at least.

"Yeah. I've been briefed on it. Recently, even." His father looked at his watch and cleared his throat. "But I'm not allowed to discuss it. Hopefully someone will call Ellen soon."

"Soon!" Nick shook his head. "No, that's not the answer you're giving me. Ellen and Susie have heard nothing. Nothing. Not even a proof-of-life or an email to let them know they aren't forgotten."

"No need to get upset." Why was that always the statement? Don't get upset. Focus on the next thing—move on.

"Damn it. No one is returning Ellen's calls. It's Christmas Eve. Their daughter just had heart surgery, and no one will call her back about her husband." This shouldn't have been that difficult to understand.

"Contacting families...not really my line of work." His father's hip beeped, but he pressed a button, silencing whatever message was coming through.

"When has that ever stopped you?" Nick moved toward the desk and put his palms on it, emotion clouding his brain as he laid it all out.

"You were the chairman of the joint chiefs of staff. The literal highest military rank. You're going to sit there and tell me you can't call in some minor favor with a representative or colonel so someone tells her Jack hasn't been forgotten?"

"There's no need to raise your voice."

"Why not!" Nick shook his head. "We're family. If you can't be vulnerable with family, then who can you be vulnerable with? Family is supposed to catch you when you fall. Supposed to stand with you when you make big life choices. Not run when you need them. Or throw them out when you choose..."

Nick cleared his throat. He was here for Ellen and Susie. And Bryn.

Bryn... Family.

He stepped back and took a deep breath. Bryn had been vulnerable with him. Let him into her heart after her ex-husband. And the first time she'd asked him to dig deep, to dig really deep about wanting his father's approval, he'd turned and run.

He'd moved on, instead of focusing on what really mattered.

"The US government doesn't deal with terrorists." His father's voice was even. No hint that Nick's outburst ruffled him at all.

Focus on this moment, then next stop, Bryn's.

"There are back doors in every policy. And last I checked, you work for a contract company now. Plausible deniability is your game. Besides, it's not like I'm asking for a rescue. Just a freaking phone call to his wife and daughter. Hell, it doesn't even have to be for Christmas. Before New Year's. Just make it happen."

"Mitch."

It was weird to hear someone call his father by his first name. For Nick's entire childhood, he'd been *General*. Nick turned to see a man standing in the doorway. He was wearing civilian clothes, but his carriage was either military or *very* recently ex-military.

"I need five minutes, Peyton."

"Don't have it. It's lockdown time."

Lockdown. No. Nick knew what that meant. No communications. Everything stayed still until whatever op was over. It was Christmas Eve. This couldn't be happening. "Dad."

His father's eyes softened for just a moment. Or maybe they didn't. "An op sped up, and I need your phone. Now."

"No." He'd done what he'd meant to. This was

not where Nick was spending Christmas Eve. He needed to get to Bryn. Needed to return her text.

"I'm leaving. At least I can tell Bryn I tried. And that I know the answer to her question."

"Who is Bryn and what question did she ask?"

"Mitch!"

"I'll be in the command room in three minutes. Everyone has their orders. Follow them."

Peyton didn't salute and he seemed less than thrilled, but he turned on his heel.

"What question?"

"She's my…was my girlfriend." The word was stung as it passed his lips. "She asked if I needed your approval. I told her of course not." There wasn't time for this discussion, and honestly, it was Bryn he wanted to have it with. "But I was wrong. I wanted you to see me. To be proud of the choices I made. But it's not what I need. Not anymore."

Bryn's smiling face floated in his memory. "I have someone that wants me for me. That sees my value." And he was going to do whatever it took to win her back.

"Mitch!" The call came from down the hall, and he saw his dad's eyes switch to the doorway.

"Stay here until this is over. Phone." He held out his hand, and Nick put the phone into it. He'd seen the look often enough to know that arguing was pointless.

His father paused at the door. "I'm glad you came. I know it doesn't seem that way."

It didn't, but he wasn't going to press his dad about it.

"It shouldn't be more than six hours. No one in or out. Can't run the risk of any leaks."

Nick had no intention of leaking anything... not that he'd get the chance. "Fine. And I don't get to know what it is?" Nick slid into the chair across from the desk. This was the worst way to spend Christmas Eve.

"Sorry. Maybe there will be a Christmas miracle." His father's words were soft, but he didn't look back this time.

Christmas miracle. Cryptic words from a cryptic man.

Nick blew out a breath. No answers on Jack, but Bryn would understand. And they'd find someone else to help them. Nick wasn't sure how, or who, but he had six hours to think it through.

Nothing to do but close his eyes and wait.

"Your father sends his regards. You're free to go." The man placed Nick's phone back into his hand, then turned and walked out of the room.

He didn't want any more family talk anyway. But to send a lackey... At least Nick could close this chapter and move on to the new one.

The most important chapter—Bryn.

"Merry Christmas." Nick muttered through

a yawn. He looked at his watch and his spirit sank. It was far too late to call Bryn or show up at her door. Which was exactly what he wanted to do. So he'd get a few hours of rest, then tell the woman he loved Merry Christmas…and that he needed her.

CHAPTER SIXTEEN

"BRYN!" THE SIGHT of her blond braid sent happiness through his exhausted brain. Honey was walking beside her on Ward 34. Reindeer antlers and a Santa sweater made them look like they'd stepped out of a holiday card.

She turned, surprise written across every part of her face. "Nick? Oh, my."

He knew he looked like hell. He'd fallen asleep as he'd waited for the clock to reach an appropriate hour. When he'd jolted awake an hour ago, all his soul had wanted was to be with her.

"Merry Christmas, Bryn."

"Merry Christmas." She rocked back on her heel. "I sent you a text yesterday."

"I know. My father confiscated my phone." That sounded wild, an actual truth-is-stranger-than-fiction situation.

"What?"

"I actually don't have a great deal to add to that. Saw my dad, pleaded for him to have someone call Ellen. Pretty sure that failed. Then some op or something started. He took my phone, and I was locked down for six hours."

Bryn's eyes were saucers, and her mouth was hanging open. "What?"

Yeah. Repeating that question made sense.

"Wildest Christmas Eve ever…and the most boring. But that's not why I'm standing here." Nick stepped closer, yearning to reach out to her.

Honey pushed her head between his legs. "It's good to see you too, Honey."

"Why are you here?"

"For you. I'm done running. You were right— I wanted my father's approval. I think I've kept moving because I didn't feel comfortable with myself. Like I wasn't enough. No matter what place I work or the achievements I get, it isn't in uniform, and he'll probably always consider me a quitter."

"You are not a quitter." Her right hand formed a fist. This woman. This brilliant, loving, beautiful person was ready to go into battle for him, even after he'd walked out.

"I know." The words were cleansing.

Her eyes roamed his face, looking for a break or a worry that he didn't mean it. The woman was a mood reader, a trauma response she couldn't help. One that she'd tried using to help him and he'd thrown in her face.

"I'm glad you know that. I really am. It's a wonderful Christmas present." Nick stepped closer, moving Honey with him. "I love you, Bryn."

Her mouth fell open, and he hated the surprise on her features. He was going to spend the rest of his life making sure that she was never again surprised by how much he cared for her.

"You're my person. I shouldn't have fled the other night. I should have called the next morning. I should—"

Her finger lay against his lips. "I love you, too." She stepped into his arms—as close as Honey would allow.

"I should have asked you for help right away, too. I was worried how you'd react."

He kissed her head, loving the feel of her in his arms. "With good reason."

"Still, you aren't my parents or Ethan. I trust you with all my feelings."

"All our feelings." Nick brushed his lips against hers. He'd needed to see her. Waiting until her shift was over had not been an option, but he wished he could seal this moment with more passion.

"Honey!" Susie's call made Bryn chuckle as she stepped back.

"It's always about Honey." Nick kissed her again, then pulled back.

"You get used to it." She wrapped an arm around his waist as Ellen wheeled Susie up.

"Merry Christmas, Susie." Bryn moved to get down on her level.

"Merry Christmas." The little one sighed as she ran a hand over Honey's coat. "I secretly asked Santa to bring Daddy home—at the window when Mommy was out. She thought I was sleeping."

"Oh, baby." Ellen rubbed her daughter's head.

"I know he isn't real, but…" She shrugged, then leaned toward Honey.

Such sad words. Maybe her dad wouldn't be home for Christmas, but Nick would find some other way. One of his siblings might know someone.

"Ho! Ho! Ho!"

Nick froze as the sound echoed behind him. He'd never heard his father make Santa noises. And he wasn't hearing it now. It couldn't be…

"Ellen. Susie!" A man with long, light brown hair pushed past Nick and Bryn.

Cries of "Jack!" and sobs filled the air as the small family reunited.

"Nick." His father's voice was right behind him.

He turned, his hand squeezing Bryn tightly. His father was here. In a Santa hat. A group of men were behind him—a few he recognized from last night.

There was an expectation that he'd speak. But Nick's synapses refused to offer him words.

"You must be Nick's dad. I'm Bryn. Welcome to Ward 34."

"How?" The simple word was difficult to force out.

The op last night. Clearly, they'd been ferreting Jack back to the States, but Nick still couldn't quite believe it.

"Some Christmas miracles are classified." His father offered a wink that actually looked jovial.

"Santa must be real!" Susie clapped as a nurse led the small family to an empty room to give them some privacy.

Bryn covered her mouth, and he saw a tear slip down her cheek.

"You got your wish." Nick kissed her temples.

"I had nothing to do with it." She let out a laugh as she squeezed his hand. "But this is the best Christmas morning ever."

"Technically, I think you were part of it, Bryn. I doubt my son would have given his speech to remind me of the importance of family without you." His father shrugged. "Jack still has to go through debriefing, and the med check is being done at this hospital. The reunion wasn't scheduled for today, but Nick reminded me that family is most important. And I think *you* had a lot to do with that."

"She had everything to do with it." Nick's heart leapt as Bryn looked at him.

"I have a small roast in my crock pot. Why don't you come to dinner with us, General?"

Nick held his breath. If his father said he was busy or unable to make it, that was fine.

His father's dark eyes, ones he knew were identical to his own, met his. "I'd love that. But, please, call me Mitch."

Another Christmas miracle.

EPILOGUE

"I'VE GOT SOMETHING for you." Bryn's giant smile was contagious.

Any worries the urge to pack his things would reappear had fled as his and Bryn's relationship progressed. The day she'd moved into his Boston apartment was still the happiest of his life, followed closely by the day they'd gotten engaged.

"A present?" It wasn't his birthday or Christmas, but Bryn loved gifting things, and he loved watching her excitement when she did.

"Sort of. It's outside." She looked at her phone, then back at him.

"Outside?" Nick looked to the window. Two years in Boston and he still didn't know which he disliked more, the steaming heat of summer or the biting chill of winter. Spring was gorgeous, though…something easy to forget as the heat seemed to radiate off the sidewalks today.

They'd treated more heat stroke this week than in his entire career. What could she have outside?

"Come on!" Bryn pulled him to the door.

"It's melting outside, sweetheart."

"I know, so we should move fast." She wagged a hand, and Honey lay back on her bed.

Too hot for Honey, but not him. All right, then.

They raced down the apartment steps. Sweat was already beading on his temple. And the woman he loved was nearly bouncing with excitement.

Stepping outside, he saw a miniature horse standing in the shade.

"Oreo and his owner, Cedric, came to say hello." Bryn waved to Cedric before petting Oreo on the head.

Nick clapped with a childlike excitement. "Oreo. The therapy horse."

"Yeah, sorry—your building has a *no mini horses* policy, so we had to do this out here. Which also means the little guy and I can't stay too long." Cedric patted the chocolate mane.

Nick understood, but just meeting the therapy horse was a dream come true.

"Bryn pointed out that with her nursing schedule, we kept missing you at Paws for Hope." Cedric smiled as Oreo let Nick rub his neck.

That was true. He'd gone several times, and it was always fun, but each time he'd hoped to meet Oreo. Running his hand over the horse's mane, Nick let out a sigh. As a child, he'd dreamed of riding, but then he'd not known little horses existed. If he had, he would have begged for one from sunup to sundown—to hell with the consequences.

"Thank you." Nick stood and shook Cedric's hand. It was too hot to make the little horse stay out, even in the shade.

"And thank you." He pulled Bryn to him, dropping a kiss onto her lips, enjoying the taste of her, the feel of her. That this was his life was a gift he'd never expected.

"There's more."

"Bryn…"

"Shush!" She pulled an envelope from her back pocket and handed it to him.

He opened it and stared at the gift certificate for riding lessons. "Bryn."

She pulled another envelope from her other pocket.

"This is too much."

She shook her head. "Nope. This one is mine. I get the bigger horse!"

"All right. But we're waiting until the heat breaks." Nick sighed. "Let's go back upstairs."

"I love you." Bryn put her hand through his.

"I love you, too."

* * * * *

*If you missed the previous story in the
Boston Christmas Miracles quartet,
then check out*

The Nurse's Holiday Swap
by Ann McIntosh

*And if you enjoyed this story, check out
these other great reads from Juliette Hyland*

Tempted by Her Royal Best Friend
Redeeming Her Hot-Shot Vet
Rules of Their Fake Florida Fling

All available now!